Beholden Duet

Zoey Ellis writes dark-edged fantasy romances described by readers as 'intensely erotic' and 'unputdownable.' A Londoner, cat mama, and proud romance and epic fantasy addict, Zoey loves possessive heroes, sexual tension that jumps off the page, and memorable, magical worlds. Visit her online home for more media and updates about her books and author journey: www.zoeyellis.com

~Also by Zoey Ellis~

Beholden Duet

A Savage Debt

A Tainted Claim

Myth of Omega

Crave To Conquer #1

Crave To Capture #2

Crave To Claim #3

Reign To Ruin #4

Reign To Ravage #5

Reign To Rule #6

Own To Obey #7

Own To Obsess #8

Own To Obtain #9

Empire of Angels

Claimed By Power #1

Ruined By Power #2

Awakened By Power #3

A Tainted Claim

Beholden Duet Book Two

ZOEY ELLIS

This book is a work of fiction. Names, characters, places, and incidents are products of the author's imagination or are used fictitiously. Any resemblance to actual events, locales, or persons, living or dead, is entirely coincidental.

A Tainted Claim, Beholden Duet Book 2

www.zoeyellis.com

Zoey Ellis Books
ISBN: 978-1-912931-33-0

First Edition: July 2020

For Gideon and Margarita

ONE

ANA

From her carriage window, Ana watched the shadowy stain of dusk take hold of the skies.

Maddoc would be in their room now, realizing she was not there as promised and that she wasn't coming. A strange feeling drifted in her chest; melancholy and forlorn clouding her thoughts as unbidden memories of him revolved in her mind. His twitching beard, the intensity of his eyes, that gritty bassy voice… The tremble in her stomach flickered, and her nipples hardened at the memory of his tongue grazing them, his hands gripping and squeezing the fleshy parts of her thighs, his groan when he lapped at her clit or sunk deep into—

"Ana?"

Stiffening, Ana glanced over at Ryden, who sat next to her in the carriage. "Yes?"

"Your father has been informed."

Ana nodded, exhaling a heavy breath. So, Father knew she had left, which meant Mother did too by now. It was strange being separated from them. She'd never been apart from them in such a drastic way before, and they'd been the steady base she'd relied on for so long, but she had to take the opportunity to strike out on her own.

Never would she have considered that her parents would lie to her, but even more unbelievable was her mother's outright admission that they wouldn't stop lying to her. After all their talks of upholding honesty and fairness, the betrayal of it cut her deeply. Her parents and Milly were the three people in the world she'd never dreamed would lie to her about anything. How was she supposed to know what was true anymore? As reluctant as she was to believe any word that had come out of Maddoc's mouth, if he'd been even half right about any deception on her parents' part, her life wasn't what she thought it was. And that gave way to another uncomfortable thought; what else was he right about?

A warm hand covered hers. "Are you all right, Ana?"

She turned to see Ryden gazing at her, concern in his blue eyes as they roamed her face. She smiled, relaxing in her seat. The one thing she could be sure of was Ryden. As her fated mate, he was the only one who was guaranteed to be there for her, to protect her and be her home, regardless of what happened. "Of course, this is just… unexpected, that's all."

"I know. It will take some getting used to." He paused, staring at her. "I was surprised you came with me."

"You were?"

Ryden nodded. "I thought you'd want to consult your parents or at least have me prove that I could do what I said."

Ana tilted her head slightly. Was he implying she was foolish for believing him without proof? Perhaps she had been. "I desperately want the promise to be broken," she admitted. "I didn't want to go back into that room to… him."

Ryden's jaw clenched. "I don't blame you."

"And I know we are fated mates, Ryden. I must have faith in that. If there's even a chance we can break the promise and be married… I have to take it, regardless of what my parents think."

A smile spread on his handsome face. "That's the way I feel, Ana."

Ana squeezed his hand, returning his smile. "Good. So tell me how we can break the promise. Both my parents were adamant it couldn't be done."

"It has to do with the majority vote of the houses," Ryden explained, leaning back in his seat. "There are five houses, as you know, and in all voting scenarios the majority wins. The houses can overthrow a decision made by the ruling couple if the majority of the houses agree."

Ana nodded. She'd heard of that concept, but slightly differently. "I thought it was only if the houses were unanimous in their decision that they could overthrow a decision by the king or ruling couple?" It rarely happened because each of the houses had such different interests, but it was possible.

"Usually yes," Ryden agreed. "But in this case, we will agree that the majority vote should count."

Unease wormed through Ana's stomach. "So it's not guaranteed we can break it?"

"It will be more likely to happen if we have public support."

Horror jumped into Ana's throat. "We're going to make it public?"

"Only if we need to, Ana," Ryden said. "But it might come to it if the other houses and the king fight us on the decision."

"But the commoners won't agree that Maddoc isn't owed the promise if he saved Father's life. They would expect him to honor it—that's been the whole reason they've been trying to keep it quiet."

"Don't panic, Ana," he said, taking her hands again. "We've got a plan and strategy that will ensure we will prevail on this. You've just got to trust me."

Ana held his gaze and took a deep breath. She had just learned that she couldn't trust her parents to be honest with her, and even though Ryden had never shown her any reason not to trust him, she was nervous about his ability to judge the situation, when Maddoc was a factor they had to consider. Ryden was from House Redcrest and very experienced in arguing politics and familiar with Allandis law. Perhaps he could see a way to get through this that she wasn't aware of? But Maddoc could not be dealt with the way the court could. "I trust you, Ryden," she said. "But you must understand that you are not only dealing with the assembly or the crown. You are dealing with Maddoc. He has no concern or respect for innocent lives, and he will drag others into this if he does not get what he's owed."

Ryden shifted uncomfortably in his seat. “Is he in love with you?”

A beam of something strange shot through the cloudiness in Ana’s stomach, but she pushed it away. “No, I don’t think so. It is about the principle. He was owed three nights, and he didn’t get it. He will think it is not honorable, and he *will* retaliate.”

“He isn’t one to determine what is or isn’t honorable considering his crimes,” Ryden barked, his eyes flashing. “It is all very well for him to murder, steal, and rape, but we are not honorable for giving him two nights out of three? That bastard cannot dictate anything to us. He is not just a nameless man or a criminal, he is the most despicable outlaw known to the kingdom. He shouldn't have been given that much power just for saving the king."

Ana’s gaze sharpened on him. "I am grateful that he did, Ryden."

Ryden met her gaze. "Ana, I know King Orick is your father, but if he was that careless while hunting, it is a sign he is losing his touch. All of his king's guard were killed or maimed, leaving him unprotected. That doesn't sound like a situation that should befall a competent king. Where were his archers? Where were his own weapons? It is well recognized that kings should take all necessary steps to protect themselves from having to be saved by anyone other than their knights."

"The men who attacked him were not from Allandis, Ryden," Ana said, grappling with the annoyance that surged in her chest. "They planned it—they must have known his schedule and attacked when he was vulnerable."

"Is there evidence of that? Did you ask your father?"

“There was evidence they carried an insignia not recognized in Allandis. I assume he would have shared that with the houses."

Ryden’s shoulders lifted. “He may have. I wouldn’t necessarily have been told everything about the incident since I’m not a formal representative of Redcrest,” he admitted. “But the fact he was attacked badly enough to owe his life to Maddoc is a disgrace.” He turned to face Ana and remained quiet for a long moment. “Ana, I know you love your father and I respect him a great deal. But it is time for you, and him, to come to terms with the fact that he is no longer fit to rule. He should step aside and let us take the throne."

Ana’s eyes widened in alarm. "Us? But we're not ready for that kind of responsibility!"

"I disagree. What your father has made you go through is inhumane. It has caused more damage to our future, our children’s future, and the future of the crown than any other single act. He is a detriment to us and himself. I don't think we should wait to succeed him." He paused, taking in Ana's panicked face. "I know that is hard to hear, but the crown isn’t just about one man, it’s about Allandis. Take some time to think about it, Ana.”

Ana could barely reply. She slumped back in her seat, a lump building in her throat. Usurping her father would be considered an act of violence. It would cause much discontent in the kingdom and wouldn’t be an easy thing to do, especially on the basis of her father being incompetent for an incident in which he was ambushed. How could Ryden use that as the sole basis for him being an unworthy king? It wasn't a wise argument to make.

She watched the buildings passing by her window without really seeing the scenery. Maddoc suggested that her father did things in court that she wasn't aware of—things that made him unlawful like Maddoc. "Do you go to many court events?" she asked after a while, still watching the skies.

"Yes, quite a few."

"What did you think of my father's decisions and approach?"

"They've been good," Ryden said hesitantly. "But that doesn't mean he should remain king in light of what happened with Maddoc."

Ana turned to him. "Would the kingdom agree?"

Ryden's expression became guarded, but he said nothing.

"Because that is what we will be fighting against," Ana explained. "The Allandis people like familiarity. My mother and father are proven leaders who have kept the kingdom stable for years—we don't have that track record. They may strongly rebel against any suggestion that we take over."

Ryden watched Ana carefully. "Did you learn that from your studies?"

Ana frowned. "Learn what?"

"About usurping and its consequences."

"Yes, and from reading."

"I thought your studies focused around history."

Ana looked at him in confusion. "All instances of usurping come from the past. What does it matter?"

Ryden was silent for a moment. "I'm not saying it will be easy, Ana. We will meet resistance, but it doesn't mean it shouldn't be done. The fact remains that the king owes a debt to Maddoc. We do not."

"But if I had gone through with tonight—"

"I didn't want you to," Ryden said sharply. "And you didn't either. It is not our burden, Ana."

Ana lowered her gaze. As her father's daughter and heir, she'd felt it *was* her burden. And maybe it had been before tonight. But as her Alpha enforcing his intention to wed her, Ryden had every right to insist that she not be involved, or at least dispute it with her. It was not unreasonable that the circumstances would upset her mate. The destruction of the crown wasn't as personal an offense as his Omega being used by another man. Now she had chosen to go with him, she'd ultimately chosen his needs and opinions over those of her father's. "I suppose not," she murmured, her gaze returning to the window.

The carriage continued its travels as the sky morphed from the muddy blue of dusk to velvety navy, encrusted with twinkling stars.

Finally, just as Ana's head drooped on Ryden's shoulder, the carriage slowed and lurched to a stop. Ryden assisted her out of the carriage and led her up to his mansion.

Ana had visited most of the royal house mansions before, when she was getting to know the families, prominent figures and their status' within Allandis, but she didn't recall Ryden's home. It was more modern and smaller than the palace, but no less grand. Each of the houses owned a castle in the kingdom, but the representatives of each house lived in mansions near the palace for when the royal assembly gathered. Even though Ryden wasn't an official representative, Redcrest was one of the wealthier houses, so it could afford to give promising dukes like Ryden such accommodation.

Ryden assisted Ana to the semidark entrance hallway before releasing her arm and heading back to the carriage to instruct his staff. Inside, a smoky, charred odor from a fireplace mingled with the tang of polish, but the building was mostly dark with only a few candles dotted along the walls. Nerves jittered in Ana's stomach. This would be her new home now, at least until she was crowned and could move back to the palace. She looked around, wondering if she could really make this place her home, but memories of Milly, her library, and her parents made it difficult to imagine... It could never be the same.

"Princess Ana."

Ana turned to see an older man leaning in a doorway that led off from the hallway. "Duke Aldous," she greeted in surprise. "What are you doing here? I didn't expect anybody to be visiting Ryden so late."

"Waiting for you, Your Majesty," Aldous said, his eyes twinkling as he raised the tankard in his hand in greeting. "I'm glad you agreed to come. We are pleased to have you onboard, Ana. Your contributions to this alliance will be invaluable."

Ana eyed his tankard, wondering if he was drunk. "We?"

Aldous gestured behind him. "The houses that have come together to support you and Ryden's efforts."

Ana's brows raised in shock. "Who else is here?"

"Come and see," Aldous said, nudging his head for her to follow him.

Ana followed him, her stomach dropping as she realized the lounge beyond the doorway held several visitors, all waiting for her and Ryden. In the low candlelight, she recognized two representatives each from houses Thorneshaw and Goldfrost. "Good evening," she said nervously. She ran her hands down her dress, wondering if she was appropriately dressed. She hadn't prepared herself in any kind of elaborate fashion to meet Maddoc for the third night, and she certainly wasn't expecting to meet several important dukes and duchesses from the royal houses.

"Good evening, Princess Ana." Duke Everard stepped forward. He stood next to Duke Theodore, both from Goldfrost. "We don't mean to alarm you, but this alliance was made at significant risk to us, and we want to be sure you are fully in agreement with what is planned. Things will commence quickly now that you have left the palace, and we will need to move swiftly. Everyone will need to play their part."

Ana blinked, looking around the room as she tried to process what he was saying. "Ryden explained the general plan in the carriage on the way here, but I would appreciate knowing what part I am to play."

Duke Everard nodded. "Of course."

"Ladies and gentlemen," Ryden greeted as he entered the room. "Let's not move too quickly and overwhelm Ana. She has just been traveling for a couple of hours to get here, after narrowly escaping a night with that savage. Let us please allow her some time to familiarize herself with her new home, or at least rest and have a drink for a moment."

"Respectfully, we do not have time for such luxuries," Duke Darcel of Thorneshaw said apologetically. He was accompanied by Duchess Rhoslyn. "The fact we are all here right now is already risky for us. Our greatest advantage is ensuring they don't know what's coming."

"Who?" Ana asked.

Ryden shot Darcel a look, and led Ana to a nearby chair. "The alliance for this particular purpose is made up of houses Redcrest, Goldfrost, and Thorneshaw," Ryden said. He turned to the rest of the room. "Firstly, I have to ask, are all the families within your houses in agreement with this?"

"We are here, aren't we?" Everard of Goldfrost said dryly.

Each royal house was comprised of three distinct families who had close ties to each other. Some families were small, others were large, encompassing uncles, nieces and cousins. The size of the family depended on the wealth of the house and how it was distributed, but each family had a representative who spoke and acted on behalf of the house. The two representatives from each house in Ryden's lounge made up the majority of their house.

"That doesn't mean your whole house is in agreement," Aldous said dryly.

"Whatever we decide, the other family will either be in support or fall in line," Everard said.

"Same with us," Duchess Rhoslyn said.

"Good." Ryden handed Ana a glass of fruit wine and she took a deep mouthful, relishing the fresh and fruity flavor. "Then we are officially in alliance, since all the Redcrest families are in agreement as well."

"When do we challenge the promise with the court?" Darcel asked. "When do we bring this alliance to the court and the people and start building momentum with this?"

"I think it's more important that Ana and I marry first," Ryden said. "Our marriage will bring more power to the situation and allow us to make more legitimate requests of the people and the crown."

"When is the quickest you can get married?" Duke Aldous asked. Aldous was Ryden's uncle, and a powerful man within the Redcrest house and the court. It was no secret that Ryden looked up to him, and Ana also liked him. He'd always been kind to Ana, visiting her and bringing gifts, and even sending her books to study. He'd always made it clear how pleased he was that Ryden had been matched with her and was the one in court who'd been aggressively arguing against Maddoc's request.

"It is possible in three or four days," Ryden said.

Ana inhaled a sharp breath. Three days until she was married?

Ryden glanced at her. "We're just bringing it forward, Ana," he said reassuringly. "Just like we discussed before we left."

Ana nodded. She wasn't sure what made her uncomfortable about the idea of marrying the man that she'd been planning to marry for years; it just seemed so final. Maybe that was a good thing. "Three days is fine."

"Use your head. We cannot wait three days before we bring the matter of the Royal Promise to the court." The growl came from Duke Theodore who was leaning against the wall by the fireplace staring out the window. His posture appeared relaxed, but the agitation in his voice rumbled around the room with force. He was known to be a difficult Alpha to please—one who wasn't concerned about politeness or etiquette. Ana had seen him rouse many Alphas into a foaming-mouthed fury by his lack of respect for them in court. "That is too much time for the king to do something," he continued, "either in court, or to collect his daughter with the full force of the crown. And we don't know what this outlaw and his mad men will do."

"If we could do it tomorrow, I would," Ryden said. "But we need to prepare the announcement tour and the ceremony. It's important no one can say it was done improperly."

Theodore lifted a shoulder. "We still must bring our argument to the court tomorrow," he said firmly. "We can announce it, we spread the word, and ask for all to attend, make a big spectacle of it that the king cannot avoid, just like Maddoc did."

"The king was intending to make a big spectacle out of Maddoc and that severely backfired," Aldous pointed out. "Are you sure this won't?"

Theodore pushed off the wall and glared at him. "That is the risk we take every time we hold court. We just have to make sure we are prepared—our argument must be strong. We need the public to agree with us."

"We could do with having a day to prepare, then," Ryden said. "It would strengthen our position. The commoners could be difficult to deal with about not honoring the promise."

"You have been arguing this since Maddoc first showed up at the court," Theodore growled. "What are you afraid of?"

Ryden matched his growl, squaring his shoulders toward him. "Nothing. It just needs to be done right."

"We don't need more time." Theodore paused for a moment. "What we need is a distraction. Your wedding announcement and tour should be enough. It needs to happen at the same time as the hearing."

Ryden frowned. "That means I cannot be in court arguing in support of Redcrest."

Theodore raised his ale, a grim grin on his face. "Then you will need to trust the rest of us."

Ryan's unease filled the silence that followed. But after a moment, his posture relaxed. "Tonight we plan our argument for the dismissal of the promise. Tomorrow we present our arguments in court and announce the wedding, and the following day Ana and I marry. Is everyone in agreement?"

A wave of nods dipped around the room while Ana looked between them. "I just want to ask Princess Ana one thing," Everard said, leaning forward toward her. "Are you aware what was agreed for our support in this."

"Now is not the time, Everard." Ryden's face darkened.

"I will not move forward unless I know the princess is fully aware of the agreement," Theodore said sharply. "We are all taking too much of a risk."

"Agreed," Everard said. "We have only tonight to confirm this alliance."

Ryden stilled. "Fine," he said, after a long moment. He turned to Ana. "I didn't want to tell you all this tonight, Ana, but it is important you know."

Ana stared up at him, her stomach souring. "What is it?"

"Once we are married, the alliance between the three houses will petition to overthrow your parents."

Ana's throat tightened. For a moment, she couldn't speak.

"And our children will need to be paired with children from Thorneshaw and Goldfrost."

"Our children?"

Ryden nodded. "Our first- and third-born to Goldfrost. Our second-born to Thorneshaw."

Ana's head spun. "But how can we decide who they are paired with? It's not up to us to decide."

"The fated mates pairing process only applies to Alphas and Omegas." Aldous stepped forward, his voice gentle. "Of course, that will not be interfered with. But if you have Beta children, or Alphas whose true mates are not identified by the age of twenty-two, they are to be matched accordingly."

Ana was unable to draw on any words. Making an arrangement with one child was one thing. But three? And if they were Betas, they wouldn't have any freedom to find partners they truly loved; they would be stuck with whomever the houses decided for them. How could she do that to her own children? As an Omega she had the security of knowing her pairing was something beyond her own decision, but her Beta children would be forced into a life that didn't guarantee their happiness—all because of this alliance.

Ana shook her head slowly as she bought her eyes up to meet the gazes on her. "How and why would you ask that of me?"

Theodore huffed out a breath, shaking his head and muttering as he turned away.

"Each child who marries into another house, strengthens our bond with that house, Ana," Ryden said. "This is how we ensure that the houses benefit from helping us."

"Helping us do what?" Ana asked, sharply. "Usurp my parents? Since when was that a priority?"

"Since they whored you out to that bastard!" Ryden boomed, his eyes flashing. "Sacrifices have to be made to ensure we can correct the damage they have done."

"And what sacrifices are you making?" Ana questioned, rising to her feet, her breath hot in her lungs. "How can you be happy about making our children miserable by forcing them to marry into other houses? How is this in their best interest? Are you not simply whoring them out the same way you accuse my parents of doing?"

A moment of stunned silence followed her outburst.

"Ana!" Ryden's face darkened as he roared her name, and the prickling rush along her arms made her hair stand on end.

Before he could say anything further, Aldous stepped in front of him. "No one will force any of your children to remain in a loveless marriage, Ana. That is not the point of this alliance."

Ana dragged her eyes from Ryden to Aldous. "Then what is the point of it?"

"Surely the princess cannot be so unaware of how things are done?" Theodore said, the grit in his voice both bitter and sarcastic. "This kind of arrangement is not unusual, Princess Ana."

"I told you to let me explain things to her," Ryden said hotly. "I don't know what she knows and what she doesn't."

"Then you should have thought of that before seeking us out to do this," Theodore said sharply. "We need her in agreement."

At that, everyone in the room quietened, and Ana stared at them all in confusion, dread fogging up her throat. There were clearly things she didn't know that they all did. Maddoc's words came flooding back to her, as did her mother's. How much didn't she know? A bracing apprehension gripped her. Nothing was how it seemed anymore—her life was built on falsehood upon falsehood. How could she know who she was if nothing in her life was the way she perceived it? And how could she possibly rule?

"We will give you tonight to rest, princess," Darcel said, gently. "I think nothing can be decided or agreed tonight."

Rhoslyn rose from her seat. "I agree with Ryden that we should have let the princess rest before discussing this. She has just been through an ordeal for the past two nights and was preparing to suffer it again today. She needs time."

"We don't have time to spare," Theodore said bluntly. "We cannot all gather again before tomorrow and we cannot move forward with our plans until this is decided. This decision is not that hard—it is common."

"Is it?" Rhoslyn said, raising a brow. She turned to the Goldfrost men in the room. "So if I arranged for a huge, violent Alpha to fuck you raw for the next two nights, you'd be in a good frame of mind to make life-changing decisions on behalf of your children immediately after?"

Aldous' laughter burst out across the room while Theodore's eyes narrowed, his entire body stiffening.

Rhoslyn didn't wait for an answer. "We will await confirmation of the princess' decision tomorrow when she visits us on the announcement tour. Court won't be until midafternoon, anyway. By the time she has visited at least one of our two houses, we will know whether or not to proceed."

Ana nodded, smiling weakly at her. She didn't think she could ever make such a decision, but everything rested on this alliance, and her Alpha had already agreed to it. She just needed to understand it.

Ryden called on a servant to take her to her room and prepare for bed, and as she rose to her feet, he kissed her forehead. "I didn't want to tell you like this. We will talk more tomorrow."

Ana nodded, but didn't respond. Somehow his words felt as empty as her mother's, and she couldn't bear another moment listening to them. As she followed the servant who wasn't Milly, into a bedchamber that wasn't her own, she blinked away the tears that had built. Maddoc had been right about a lot of things so far, but she wouldn't let him be right about her. She wasn't a puppet for anyone. And as soon as she'd rested, she'd address her concerns with this alliance.

❖

Humid heat encased her whole body, and a solid weight pinned her to the bed. Ana sighed, relishing the peaceful security underneath her Alpha. But as her consciousness awakened, her eyes flickered open. Everything smelled wrong. And the feel of his flesh on hers was… uncomfortable.

Stiffening, Ana tilted her head to see Ryden on top of her, his arms wrapped firmly around her body, securing her to him. An intense panic rose before she even recognized it. Thrashing, writhing, and twisting as hard as she could, she tried to get out of his hold, but the dead weight of an Alpha was no simple thing for an Omega to shift. Soon, her increasingly desperate movements woke him with a growl. "What is it?"

He lifted himself a little off the bed, and Ana scooted out from under him, scrabbling to the edge of the bed on all fours, breathing hard as the panic made her heart thump in her ears.

"What, Ana?" Ryden growled in annoyance.

Ana grabbed the sheets with her fists and forced herself to still. Panting, she tried to answer, but couldn't speak.

Ryden watched her. "Ana?"

"Nothing," Ana finally said, her breathing calming. "I just felt… You were on top of me and…" Her words faded away. How could she tell him that his scent was all wrong? That the feel of his body wasn't right? That the muscles along his chest and arms were not the ones she wanted pressing her down, cuddling her or rubbing on her bare skin? How could she tell him she wasn't comfortable underneath him? He was supposed to be her mate.

Ryden watched her, his frown deepening. "Ana. You belong with me."

"I know," Ana said, even though the idea of it made her tense. "It's just…"

When she didn't continue, Ryden leaned forward slowly and reached for her, monitoring her carefully as he moved closer.

Ana could not stop tensing, digging her nails harder into the bed the closer he came. She desperately did not want to be touched. When his thumb grazed her cheek, tears sprung to her eyes, and Ryden growled in annoyance. Moving swiftly, he hooked his arm around her waist and pulled her down to the bed and underneath him.

Ana forced herself not to squeal as her back hit the bed. Ryden loomed over, brushed his hand up her leg, and hooked an arm under her knee.

Ana slapped a hand on his chest in alarm. "Ryden, what are you doing?

"You have to get past what happened, Ana," Ryden growled. "You only have the memories of him. You need to create fresh memories with me." Before she had a chance to respond, he lowered his body and crushed his mouth on hers.

The kiss was rough and insistent, his hot breath and his warm mouth smothered her, his tongue seeking entry, and for a moment Ana allowed herself to experience it with him. But within a few moments the uncomfortable feeling returned full force, suffocating her and forcing her panic to resurface.

She dragged her mouth away and tried again to claw away from him, fighting as her breathing increased.

"Ana!" Ryden growled as he let her scramble away again. "It won't be like with him."

Ana kept her head low and nodded, taking a deep breath before raising her eyes to him. Maybe that was what she was afraid of. "I just need time, Ryden" she said, almost pleading. "Please give me time to get used to being close to you. My first sexual experience was with him and… I just need time."

Ryden's eyes flashed. "You are my mate. I will not have you withdrawing from me."

Ana's mouth tightened at his tone. "Yes," she remarked bitterly. "We have to get on with our breeding duties to pay for this alliance, don't we?"

He moved so quickly she didn't even have time to yelp before he grabbed her and threw her onto the bed.

"I allowed your comments last night because I understood you were distressed." Ryden's contorted features made him look like a different man—still beautiful, still Ryden, but sinister. Fear crept into Ana's chest as she stared up at him. "But you will not use that tone with me again, Ana. I don't know what happened during those nights with him—I'm sure you screamed and fought and withdrew from *him*. But you will not behave that way with me. You will be respectful of me. Do you understand?"

Ana nodded, her eyes wide.

The anger seeped from Ryden's eyes and he relaxed his grip on her. "You are the perfect princess," he murmured, his voice slightly softer. "And we are a perfect match. We just need to overcome the difficult start we've had." He lowered his mouth onto hers again, and this time Ana tried to kiss him back. She had to at least try to spark the feelings she knew were there for him. Squeezing her eyes tight and ignoring all the alarm signals in her body telling her something was wrong, she pressed her lips back against his. But eventually she couldn't help but wrench her mouth away and turn her head to the side.

Ryden lifted up, watching her for a long moment, a blend of annoyance and resignation in his eyes. He moved to sit on the edge of the bed. "If you need time, you can have time," he said, his voice low. "But on our wedding night there will be no more abstinence between us, Ana." He looked at her. "I will take what I need from my mate. Do you understand?"

She nodded, trying to control the fear building in her throat. To some degree she understood his anger—she had already been with another man when he had been waiting for her, and now she was pulling away from him, acting like she couldn't stand his touch. No mate would be happy with that. She couldn't imagine Father being at all happy if Mother behaved that way with him.

But what really concerned her was the reaction to his touch. It was strange to react that way with her own mate. She couldn't recall feeling that way about Maddoc, and while she didn't want to compare them, she had nothing else to go by. She'd been looking forward to her experience with Ryden's touch eradicating memories of Maddoc, but how could it if she couldn't bear to even kiss him? Maybe it really was trauma.

Ryden stood and grabbed his clothes. "Have you had time to think about the agreement with the alliance?"

Ana relaxed on the bed. "No, but I don't understand why it's necessary."

"Because the houses need guarantees that they will get something out of helping us," Ryden said as he dressed. "And marrying into the ruling family raises the status of their houses."

When Ana looked at him blankly he continued with a growl.

"You know the houses are not all equal, surely?"

"Yes, I know," she replied, almost indignantly. "Redcrest and Sterling are the wealthiest."

"Right. And greater opportunities to grow that wealth come from having a pleasant relationship with the crown. Whether it is a son or daughter who is king or queen, or simply a good history of positive and profitable dealings, all houses want to be on good terms with the crown." He tilted his head. "I am surprised you are unaware of this."

"I *do* know this," Ana insisted. "But I thought it was a joint, amiable effort. I didn't realize it was combative until recently."

"Well, it is," Ryden said bluntly. "Very combative. It has been that way for generations." He paused. "Haven't you noticed the tension in court?"

"I noticed that the houses hardly ever agree," Ana said. "And I noticed it can get very heated between them"—in truth it had even become physically violent on rare occasions—"but I didn't realize it extended beyond that."

Ryden gave her a wry look. "What you see in court is the *mildest* expression of the true tension between us."

Ana's eyes widened. "Oh."

"Disputes run deep and some have existed for decades. Have you noticed that some houses are always in agreement and others are not?"

Ana nodded. "Sterling and Redcrest never agree."

"Right," Ryden said. "But Goldfrost and Sterling always do."

"They have an alliance?"

"Not exactly. Sterling owns a lot of land Goldfrost has built on."

Ana lifted her head in understanding. "So they are always under threat if they provoke Sterling."

"Yes." Ryden leaned forward, bracing his hands on the bed. "So Goldfrost agreeing to side with us in court today, against Sterling *and* the crown, will put them at great risk."

Ana thought back to Theodore and Everard's agitation and insistence the night before.

"But they will take that risk if it is guaranteed that two of our Beta children will marry into Goldfrost and Thorneshaw."

Ana examined his face. "You think it's worth it to offer our children for their support?"

"I do." Ryden's expression and tone was firm. "It is not unusual. Almost all Betas in the royal assembly marry through arrangement across the houses. You may not have noticed because there is never a need for the details to be announced, and your own pairing hasn't happened that way, but it is extremely common."

Ana exhaled slowly as she thought. So this was the true barter system used among the royal assembly. She'd simply been lucky to be born an Omega with the guarantee of being paired with her fated mate.

"When we visit the houses on our announcement tour today," Ryden said, slow and steady, "you will locate a representative of Goldfrost and Thorneshaw and tell them you are in agreement with the terms."

Ana met his gaze. "And if I don't?"

"Then you will be left to the mercy of your father, or more likely, the outlaw, because I won't be able to rid you of the Royal Promise without the assistance of the other houses." Ryden reached out and brushed her cheek with his fingers. "I told you to trust me, Ana, and you can. I wouldn't agree to something like this unless it was necessary. And it's not as though we will lose our children, they will still be ours—they will only be married when they are of age. And we can help them through it."

Ana's heart sunk as she realized there was no way to get out of agreeing to this. She had, in fact, already unwittingly consented to it when she agreed to leave the palace with him. She hadn't insisted on knowing the full terms before she left, so now her only options were to continue with the path she set herself on, or suffer the path others wanted to choose for her—Maddoc's and his wrath, or her parents' and their lies.

Ryden's touch turned firmer, and his hand curled around her jaw. "I want to hear you say you are in agreement, Ana."

Ana battled with the gloom that crept into her. "And there is no way to amend the agreement later or change it?"

"No."

Her voice came out as a whisper. "I agree."

"Good." Ryden stroked her cheek again, and Ana forced herself not to pull away from his touch. He pushed off the bed as he straightened. "Be ready to leave within the hour."

Ana watched him as he walked into the washroom, trying to process what had just happened. The conversation had revealed much about the true nature of the royal houses and the part she would now play among them. Offering her children up wasn't comfortable, but she had to trust Ryden. If the houses regularly traded marriages between them, she couldn't blame him for thinking she would be fine with it. She had to accept that she still had things to learn, and this was another piece of information she had never known.

She stared at the washroom where Ryden was. The biggest concern for her was her lack of physical connection to Ryden. If even significant hardship arose, she should be able to handle it as long as her fated mate was with her, but the attraction between them was nonexistent, while at the same time, the forlorn longing at the memories of Maddoc lingered.

Sighing, she got up from the bed and tried to shake off the unease. She had one more day until her wedding, and she had to get rid of these feelings by then.

Two

MADDOC

Maddoc stared at Duke Ryden's mansion as the sky brightened. He'd stood at the window all night watching the house, a vicious fury pulsing throughout his body, urging him to move—to do something about the fact that his Omega was in another man's possession. But if he moved, even just one inch, the fury would overcome him and no doubt spoil the plans that were being put into place to get her back. He couldn't risk that. Nothing was more important than getting Analisa back to him. And yet, his fury could not be quelled by such logic or reason. Especially not when this fucking duke had *touched* her while escorting her into his mansion.

"Maddoc." Raine's voice was annoyingly matter-of-fact. "You should eat something."

He didn't need to glance down to know she was holding a bowl of food. "I need nothing but a report on my Omega, Raine. If you cannot provide that, find someone who can."

"We have servants in the mansion, but we won't get a report from them for the next few days. You know that."

Unfortunately, the extensive land that surrounded Duke Ryden's mansion made it difficult to monitor and observe the building without alerting his sentries. The closest they could get was the servant homes on the edge of the grounds, and luckily more than one of the families supported Maddoc and his cause. As soon as he'd left the palace, Maddoc had sent instructions to his guild to set up central operations in the nearest servant house so he could monitor Ana's movements while they made their plans. But once he saw her and the duke, he hadn't moved from the window.

"We may be able to get a message from Elizabeth when she goes in tomorrow," Raine continued, gesturing to the next room where one of the residents were, "but not sooner than that."

"It's not good enough." Maddoc's low growl burned the back of his throat. "I want to know what the fuck she was doing all night. And I want to know *today*!" The fury in him roiled at the thought she might have been anywhere near the duke last night. Thankfully, her heat wasn't due for weeks. If there were any chance of it arriving while she was in the duke's possession, he would have stormed in and collected her, regardless of the consequences—though those consequences would likely include the opportunity to kill the duke.

"We've always been very careful not to betray those who provide us with information," Raine said carefully. "We've never asked them to do anything that will reveal their allegiance with us. It may be they

are unable or unwilling to give us that information—
”

The harsh growl in Maddoc’s throat cut off her words. There was no point explaining that none of that mattered now. He was on the edge of a cliff of sanity, ready to descend into the most mindless, violent rage if anyone breathed the wrong way.

Raine must have read something in his silence because she changed the subject. “I heard from Walrick. The king has called on his royal court to meet after the public court hearing opens today. They will be planning how to get the princess.”

Maddoc nodded slightly without taking his eyes off the mansion. He’d initially said he wanted to be at the palace, learning the king’s plan to do to get Ana back in order to ensure he got to her first. But realistically, he couldn’t go anywhere until his rage subsided.

Although he knew Ana was betrothed, he’d never once considered that he’d have to see her with a man other than her guards or her father. His plan had worked well—there was no reason to believe that things would fall apart on the third night and this would be a possible outcome. But he hadn’t accounted for Ana being so beautifully willful. He knew the duke wasn’t forcing her to do this—she would never have left her parents unless she wanted to; it had given him hope that her eyes were finally opening. But she was supposed to be with *him* when that happened. Her being with the duke made this about more than just the deal he made with the king about who would get her first. The need to get Ana back swirled throughout his body like a bitter, brutal whirlwind battering his insides, and it muted everything else.

Quiet footsteps behind them drew Raine's attention, and she moved away, leaving him to sink back into the dark tension of his fury. At the same time, a flurry of movement sprung up in the courtyard.

Lifting his magnifying lens, Maddoc watched in the dreary morning light as a carriage came to a stop in the courtyard. Footmen and other staff flurried around it, checking the wheels and the horses, installing cushions, blankets, and a hamper. It wasn't the kind of carriage used for a quick trip or to transport goods; it was a carriage fit for royalty. Analisa was going somewhere.

Maddoc's mood shifted a little. Maybe he could capture her while she traveled. When he turned, he caught the end of the conversation between Raine and the servant who had arrived.

"—and so they intend to do that all day."

"Do what?" Maddoc shot at him.

The man started, suddenly tense with Maddoc's eyes on him. "Visit all the royal houses. They're announcing their wedding and doing the tour."

Maddoc turned back to look at the house, his mind in deep thought. Taking Ana while she toured the houses would be extremely difficult. The chances of escaping cleanly would be low.

The good thing was, if they were traveling, it was unlikely Ryden would have much opportunity to be too inappropriate with her. Of course, if it had been Maddoc, he would be between her legs for every moment on the journey between each house, but Ryden was the type of Alpha who wouldn't turn up to any royal house with a woman who looked well fucked. Not even a beautiful, irresistible Omega. Still, he had to know if he'd dared to touch her.

Lifting his lens again, he watched for them. The sun was bright in the sky by the time Ana stepped out of the mansion, and what a sight she was. Her sleek red hair spilled over her shoulders, and her satiny blue gown clung to her incredible figure. Duke Ryden stepped out after her, and Maddoc's fury flared, his grip on his lens tightening. But as he watched them walk to the carriage and Ryden help her inside, his anger melted down to a smoldering irritation. They didn't fuck. It was clear for anyone to see. They weren't comfortable with each other the way they should be if they'd been intimate. Hell, Ana shouldn't even be able to walk properly if the Alpha who'd been betrothed to her for years had finally gotten to her last night. As the carriage began to move, he saw she was even angled away from the duke, a significant distance between them on the bench.

Maddoc lowered his lens and exhaled heavily. The duke hadn't touched her yet, but that wouldn't last. There was no Alpha who could resist an Omega in his possession for very long. It was likely that he would wait until their wedding night, but he would have her by then.

He put down his lens and moved away from the window. If Ana and Ryden were in the public eye, traveling for most of the day, he didn't need to keep an eye on her so closely. "I want their full route," he said to Raine, pointing at Ana's carriage. "And a note of any stops or deviations they make in between the houses." He headed to the door. "I'm going to the palace."

❖

“They are out of their fucking minds!” Orick stormed into his throne room, followed by the queen and the rest of his court.

Maddoc remained still, careful not to draw any attention to the wall of decorative lattice that ran along the very top of the room. The secret corridor behind it was one of the few places that allowed him to remain hidden with no disguise, even though his view was partially obscured. The most important thing was being able to listen in on one of the most important rooms in the palace.

“What are they trying to prove by this?” Orick thundered, pacing in front of his throne, as his court took their usual positions. “They are harming her more than they are helping her!”

“The commoners will never look at her the same again,” the queen murmured as though in pain. “After everything we have done to try to keep this from them… it was all in vain."

Maddoc allowed himself a grim smile. The rumors that had been circulating since his visit to the court had been confirmed by three of the houses announcing it to the commoners today and accusing the king of allowing it to happen. It had been a lively hearing, one that painted him as the ultimate villain and Ana as a pure, virginal innocent victim whom the king had not protected.

"Her reputation may be marked to some degree," one of the king’s courtiers said. "But if you recall, when we were discussing the repercussions of the outlaw’s hearing, we did suggest that Duke Ryden still marrying her would curb some of that damage to her reputation. If they are announcing their wedding, even though they claim she was harmed by you, it absolves her reputation further. The commoners may be concerned at the beginning of all this, but as long as Ana and Ryden wed successfully, no one will even remember the slight on her reputation within a year or two."

"Yes," another older courtier said. "This hearing was orchestrated to damage *you,* Your Majesty, not her."

Orick slowed to a stop. "To blame me for Ana's virginity being given to the outlaw?"

The queen inhaled sharply. "To take the throne." Her strangled voice echoed across the large room.

Orick remained still for a moment, as did the whole room. "That is why three of the houses were in agreement."

"Yes. They want to claim you are incompetent so you can be removed," she said.

A moment of silence hung in the air.

"Ana is not ready to rule, and neither is Ryden," Orick said, his voice tight. He made his way to his throne and sat down. "If they try to and I resist, what will be the consequences of that? Will they attempt to violently usurp me? What manpower could they possibly use against the crown?"

"Not necessarily, Your Majesty." The king's formal adviser finally spoke up. "It is likely they will simply claim that you are an unfit king, and that Ana needs to step in now."

"On what basis?" Orick thundered. "I have been an exemplary king, almost every single king from my line has ruled this kingdom, and have maintained a peaceful existence for all. By what reasoning could they have that I am unfit?"

"The outlaw," the queen said through gritted teeth, bitterness strong in her tone. "You owe a Royal Promise to him. That is the one thing attributed to you and none of your royal line."

"It is still risky for them to pin everything on you honoring the Royal Promise, Your Majesty," the formal adviser said. "You didn't go against Allandis Law or the expectations of the people. It is the wedding that is going to be the problem. Once she is married, they have an immediate claim to the throne without any of the other houses having a chance to interfere. They just need to find a way to remove you."

"They?" The queen's voice was sharp. "Are you suggesting my Ana has anything to do with this plan? Because she has no desire to be queen right now."

"No, of course not," the adviser said. "But we do know Duke Ryden is very ambitious, Your Majesty."

Orick nodded gravely. "And if they have the support of two other houses, it is likely they have a hand in it as well."

Maddoc ground his teeth. They were all using Analisa for their own purposes, just like her parents had done.

"So what do we do?" the queen asked, her voice stern. "How do we stop the wedding and get Ana back home with us."

"I'm not sure you can, Your Majesty," the adviser said apologetically. "She is officially an adult and she has been betrothed to a royal house for years, which means they have a small amount of claim over her.

Unfortunately, the situation does not lend itself easily to your favor with regards to Allandis law."

"I don't give a fuck about Allandis law. She is my daughter!"

Maddoc grinned at the queen's outburst. She may act virtuously regal in public, but in the privacy of her court, she was just as coarse and corrupt as the rest of them.

"Atara." Although the king spoke sternly, there was a gentleness in his tone that calmed the queen. She placed her hands in her lap and leaned back on her throne.

The king addressed the adviser. "Maddoc is going after Ana. Regardless of what the houses are trying to do with the throne, the only way to save Ana from him, and the Royal Promise, is for us to get to her first. The houses should be told about the deal I made with him—it will keep Ana safe if we can all protect her."

"I don't think the houses will care about that now, Your Majesty," another courtier said. "Goldfrost and Thorneshaw have already made their allegiances known. They cannot back down from targeting the crown."

"Then we just have to take her," the king growled, rising from his throne. "At the wedding."

The general of the king's guard stepped forward. "We can plan that right now, Your Majesty. We know where and when it will be, and we can prepare for Maddoc and his men."

"Do it." The king looked back at the adviser. "I want the houses punished for attempting this. Find a way to do it."

The adviser nodded, but his face was grim. “Will Ana still be marrying into Redcrest?”

Orick was quiet for a moment. “What are the repercussions if she doesn’t?”

The queen leaned forward and touched his arm. “It is well known Ryden is her mate. We cannot separate them.”

The king exhaled heavily and nodded.

For the next hour, the king and his royal court discussed his continued reign, how they would take Ana back, and the effect of the current circumstances on the houses relationship with the crown.

Maddoc listened to their plans, and formulated plans of his own, trying to push back his disgust at the way they were intending to continue using Ana. He would be glad to finally get her away from them—they’d already damaged her enough.

By the end of their meeting, the king decided to take her back after she married Ryden, and force Redcrest to fall in line, and that suited Maddoc fine. He planned to take her before she married. If possible, he would take her tonight and leave these warring men to their own devices.

Finally, the court dispersed to prepare their plans, leaving Orick and Atara alone in the room.

"We will get her back, Atara," Orick murmured as he took her hands in his. “And she will understand. We just need to explain things to her, that's all."

"She is rebelling." Atara’s voice was raspy. "She knows that we haven't been truthful with her and this is her way of lashing out. She has always been so calm and so obedient… It was bound to happen eventually."

"It wasn't," the king growled. "She never would have had any of these reactions or tempers if it wasn't for that bastard. He is the one who upset the balance here, not us."

"And you have to wonder," the queen murmured thoughtfully, "if that's what he had always intended to do."

Maddoc held his breath as a long silence filled the room. It wasn't possible for the ruling couple to figure out his plan, but they knew by now that he was not stupid. If Ana had truly told them some of the things she had spoken about with him, they would know that he was leading her toward topics that they would not approve of. If they stopped thinking about their throne so intensely and instead thought about why he'd done what he had, they might figure it out. But he knew they wouldn't.

"No, he said he had nothing to do with the attack on me," Orick said finally. "If that truly was a random occurrence, how could he know to be there in order to intervene and be owed a promise?"

The queen was silent for a moment. "That is assuming a lot, Orick. Those men may not have been from Allandis and they may have had nothing to do with Maddoc, but he took advantage of the situation and benefited from everything that happened. It's too much of a coincidence. I don't know how he was involved, but he is. Do not underestimate him."

Maddoc's beard twitched. It was too late for that.

❖

It took a while to leave the palace undetected. When he returned to the safe house, Maddoc was pleased

Ana had not yet returned. According to their spies out in Allandis, it seemed she was spending a couple of hours at each house and still had two more to go. They wouldn't be back at Ryden's mansion before dusk.

Maddoc discussed the king's plans with his commanders. Most of his men held the required skills needed and were already on the mainland of Allandis, but there were a few specialists he would have to call upon, and it would be a rush for them to get there. He would also need a way to disappear into the 'shire without being followed.

"We can't do it tonight, Doc," Bram concluded finally.

Maddoc growled his displeasure, but Bram just shrugged.

"It's impossible." He popped one end of a twig into the corner of his mouth. "We won't have the manpower 'til tomorra', we won't have our herd of guild 'orses or the right weaponry 'til then neither. And the way that mansion is protected, we won't get far if we try for 'er tonight." Bram used to help farmers with ailing crops turn their stock around, but when the crown deemed him nameless, he lost everything he owned. Now, he was Maddoc's most experienced and trusted strategist, and though he had his quirks, Maddoc had learned it was wise to listen to him.

Bram squinted and looked at the map again, chewing his twig. "I say we get 'er at the weddin' gardens. Easy to get in, easy to get out, easy to get lost and stay lost."

"The king will try to get her then too," Griff reminded him. Griff, another nameless man, was an older Alpha who'd once been a knight. He was

Maddoc's second-in-command. "We have to prepare for that."

"Yeah, but afterward," Bram pointed out. "*We* are snatchin' her before."

"And they will be expecting something—"

Maddoc turned away and let his commanders talk it over, returning to the window to struggle with his growing irritation. If it had to happen tomorrow, that was just one more night without Ana. And another night with her in Ryden's possession.

"Are you all right, Maddoc?"

He glanced over to see Raine. "I'm going to the mansion."

Raine stiffened. "That's not a good idea. Even if you're not caught and detained, you're too conspicuous." She waved her hands at his body to make a point about his size. "They will know you're nearby and planning something. It will make things harder for us tomorrow."

"I want to know what's going on in there," he demanded.

Raine pursed her lips and was silent. Too silent.

Maddoc frowned. "What is it?"

"Elizabeth was able to go in and report back to us since they have been out all day."

Maddoc turned to her. "And?"

"They are sharing a room, Maddoc," she said reluctantly. "And a bed."

A growl blazed from his throat and chest as his fury reignited.

"But there was no indication of…" Raine stumbled over her words. "She changed the sheets and it doesn't seem like anything happened."

Nothing happened? There was no doubt Ryden had touched Ana if they were sharing a bed.

Raine's voice was soft when she spoke again. "Maddoc, if you want company tonight—"

"Leave."

Maddoc grabbed his magnifying lens and turned toward the window, toward the mansion, back on the brutal edge of his rage. He only had to control it for one more night.

THREE

ANA

Ana remained in an unsettled state of confusion for the whole day.

The more she pondered what Ryden told her about the houses, the more things made sense. It was why certain families were always seen together and others weren't. It was why the rife gossip and speculation that high society thrived almost always centered around members of the houses or the nobles associated with them. This new awareness shone a bright light on everything Ana had originally thought, and as she toured each house, it was like she was seeing them for the first time.

At Goldfrost and Thorneshaw, she met privately with Everard, Theodore, Darcel and Rhoslyn to confirm she was in full agreement with the alliance. They were all visibly relieved, but the uneasy feeling that she was letting down her future children never left her. Unfortunately, that wasn't the only thing on her mind.

During their tour, Ryden was very affectionate. He held her hand, brushed her shoulder, pressed his hand against the small of her back, rested his hand on her hip and even kissed her forehead, and each time Ana expected her body to flourish and ripple with pleasure the way it had with Maddoc—to tingle and tremble in all kinds of delicious ways. But it didn't happen with Ryden, and over the course of the day she grew concerned.

Was she under too much stress because of what had happened recently? Maybe Ryden was under a lot of stress too and his pheromones couldn't affect her the way they were supposed to. But the more excuses she came up with, the more she remembered her parents. Regardless of what was happening around them, they remained attracted to each other; in fact, during times of stress, they sought out each other for comfort. More than once, she'd seen her mother curled in her father's lap, with him rocking her as they talked about various problems that they were dealing with—the contact comforting them both. It couldn't be stress affecting her response to Ryden.

The knot in her stomach grew as the day progressed, particularly when she realized she only had one more night until their wedding night. What if her physical response to him didn't change? Even though she had been forced to spend nights with Maddoc, she had been aroused each time, even when he had grabbed her roughly and touched her however he wanted. The idea of Ryden touching her made her want to shrink away, and that confused her. Something was wrong.

While those thoughts revolved, Ana went through the motions of the announcement with the houses; gifts were given, compliments were made, and empty promises were hinted at. She kept the smile on her face the whole time, playing the part she had been brought up to play by her parents. Except this time it felt… odd. She felt different and out of place. Only two nights ago she'd spread her legs for one of the most feared and despised men known to the kingdom, found bliss humping on his cock and screamed for more. Since then, it felt as though something inside her was broken, and the rest of her reality was fracturing too.

As they arrived at the final royal house on the tour Ana pushed all other thoughts out of her mind. The knowledge that House Sterling was so combative with the house she was marrying into made her nervous. Even Ryden was quiet in the carriage on the way there.

Once inside, the visit didn't feel like the other houses. The display of wealth was almost obnoxious, and though everyone made all the right noises and said the right words, a hint of something unsavory tinged the air. Gazes lingered on her too long, and conversation stopped or changed when she moved into earshot.

Keeping an eye on Ryden for a signal of when they would be leaving, Ana forced herself to sip her wine and smile at the women standing around her pretending to be polite, but her mind drifted back to Maddoc, and her nipples began to tingle. She had to wonder whether Betas had the same experience of sex as Omegas and Alphas. Could anyone in the room even understand that kind of intense feeling—uncontrollable, raw, carnal, distinctive?

Then she remembered. There was.

Ana glanced around, looking for the Omega that lived here. She couldn't recall her name, though she could remember what she looked like when she attended the Omega session a few years ago.

"Let's not crowd the princess, Ladies," a smooth voice called out

Ana turned to see Duchess Heloise approaching her, and she froze in place, her whole body tensing. Heloise was known to be one of the most outspoken, rude, and ruthless members of the entire royal assembly. Her eyes were quick and her tongue sharp, even though she seemed unassuming and always held a smile on her face. In court, Ana always winced when Heloise stood to debate or discuss anything—she'd even been rude to Father more than once.

"Congratulations, Princess," the duchess said, flicking her hand to dismiss the other women standing around Ana. "It's so rewarding to see our perfect princess on the eve of her wedding day. You have so much to look forward to, but I'm sure you are tired of talking about the wedding." Her eyes sparkled. "I am curious about why it has suddenly been moved forward. Nothing to do with the Royal Promise, I hope."

Ana's heart began to pound, but she kept herself relaxed. She had been expecting something like this. "My wedding has been planned for years, Duchess. Bringing it forward a few weeks is nothing remarkable. I would simply like to enter my twenty-second birthday as Ryden's wife and mate."

"I can believe that," the duchess said, pursing her lips. "But I'm not as foolish as a commoner." Her eyes narrowed slyly. "Tell me about your nights with the outlaw. I'm sure they were very… interesting. A big, hulking Alpha like that, I'm sure much happened in that room." She leaned forward. "And I'm sure Duke Ryden is upset about it? Is that why the wedding was moved forward?"

For a moment Ana couldn't speak. What was she supposed to say to such direct questioning?

The duchess lowered her voice. "You didn't say the outlaw's name while you were with Ryden did you? Alphas can be so territorial."

Ana took a slow sip of her wine, ignoring the heat that flushed her cheeks. If she said the wrong thing, her words would be twisted out of context and Ryden's reputation would be affected. She thought back to her father and his time in front of the court. How would he deal with it? She just didn't know. Taking a breath, she thought back to her conversation with Ryden that morning, and a sharp realization came to her. "I don't know that I've ever given the impression that I engage in idle gossip, Duchess," she said, keeping her voice light. "I don't. And I don't appreciate any mention of the outlaw in my presence, for obvious reasons."

The duchess' smile faded, and a fierce glare bloomed in her eyes.

"I thought that, this being my wedding announcement, the houses would try to endear themselves to me, not offend me and have me find any reason to exclude them from favorable treatment by the crown when I am queen."

The duchess' glare hardened, and her body stiffened, her hands clasping her glass tight enough to make the tips of her fingers white.

"Is that what you wish for? Are you trying to find ways to offend me, Duchess?" Ana asked the question purposefully slowly like she'd seen Father do, then she tilted her head as if pondering her own words.

"No, Your Majesty." The duchess spoke with formality but through gritted teeth. "I apologize."

Ana smiled. "Good." She glanced around. "I'm looking for the Omega that lives in this residence, do you know where I can find her?"

At that, the duchess' smile returned. "Yes, of course." Raising a hand, she called over a servant. "Take Princess Ana to see Leoma."

Ana gave the duchess an obvious fake smile. "Until next time," she said in farewell.

The duchess returned the smile, with one just as fake. "I look forward to our next talk, Your Majesty."

Ana followed the servant through the crowded room to double doors on the other side. They headed up a wide, winding staircase until they reached the floor above, then traveled through another wing before coming to a halt outside cream doors with golden handles.

Knocking loudly, the servant waited for a call before opening the door. "Introducing Princess Ana," he announced before stepping back and allowing her through.

Highly decorated with plush seats, chandeliers, furniture, and golden fittings, the room was an extravagant show of wealth. In the center a young woman sat on a wide soft bench, dressed just as elaborately as the women downstairs. Leoma was outfitted in a maroon gown, heavy jewelry, and her curly cinnamon-colored hair was wound up in a sophisticated plait. Ana was surprised how mature she looked from when she'd last seen her, but they had all been younger.

Excitement burst onto Leoma's face as soon as she saw Ana, and she jumped up from her seat. She paused, as though she had only just remembered she was wearing a dress and then lifted her skirts so she could walk quickly.

"Princess Ana," she almost squealed. "It's such a pleasure to see you again. I cannot believe that you requested to see me!" She stopped in front of Ana, seemingly unsure what to do. She curtsied and then held her hand out awkwardly, but Ana smiled and took both of her hands in her own.

"Of course I'd want to see you," she said. "Why wouldn't I?"

Leoma grinned and squeezed her hand. "You are the princess who is going to be queen. What use would you have to see me again?"

Ana laughed. "You're one of the only two Omegas I know," she said. "That's why. We have something unique in common. It's a shame we don't get to see each other more often."

Leoma turned and gestured to the chairs. "Would you like to sit?"

Ana shook her head. "I'm not going to be up here very long," she said apologetically. "I'm sure someone will notice I'm missing." She glanced around the room again. "Why aren't you downstairs with the rest of them?"

Leoma pushed out her lips. "I am to be brought down to greet you in about an hour. I'm not allowed to mingle too freely."

Ana almost rolled her eyes. "I know that feeling. Being pushed and prodded into various scenarios and being told how to act or what you can do."

"It so restricting. I cannot even imagine how it must be for you."

Ana shrugged. "I got used to it from a very young age, it's normal to me now." Her voice lowered to a murmur as she spoke, remembering all the times she had sat in her bedroom waiting to be announced to some official or important member of yet another house. "Don't worry, I won't tell anybody that I've seen you beforehand, though Duchess Heloise is the one who asked a servant to bring me here."

Leoma rolled her eyes and then tensed as though caught doing something wrong. "I don't mean to be disrespectful toward Heloise," she said hurriedly. "She is my aunt, after all. It's just… I have been disagreeable with her of late, and she doesn't appreciate it."

Ana almost laughed, but the sadness settled in her stomach. Ana had been fortunate that she didn't have to deal with royal house politics as she grew up. And even so, she'd still had the same demeanor as Leoma—afraid to offend and eager to please.

"So why did you want to see me?" Leoma asked. "I'm not very experienced in wedding announcement ceremonies. I cannot believe you get to marry Ryden! He's the best-looking Alpha in the royal assembly." Suddenly her face dropped and she slapped her hand over her mouth in shock, her eyes wide on the princess.

"It's all right," Ana laughed. "I've known Ryden for a long time now; it doesn't seem like that much of a big deal." She ignored the sinking feeling in her stomach that she shouldn't be starting her marriage with such a lack of excitement about her husband.

"Oh," Leoma breathed, relief on her face. "Sterling women would be upset about me saying that about their betrothed—I think it's because I'm an Omega and they think every man wants me." She rolled her eyes. "It's just Ryden does seem really nice and kind. And he deals with Heloise in a way I've rarely seen anyone do before, so that has to count for something."

Ana's brows lifted. "What you mean? Do they talk often?"

"I'm not sure. The last time I saw them both was when they came to visit me."

"When was that?"

Leoma pouted as she thought. "A couple of days ago, I think? It was completely out of the blue, and I couldn't figure out why they'd both come."

Ana stared at her. If Sterling and Redcrest were so against each other, why would Ryden and Heloise be making visits together? "What did they say?"

"They just asked me how I was doing in my lessons and what I'd been studying. Heloise asked me if I'd been paying attention to court events, my understanding of politics in the court assembly, how I was doing in my lessons, and what I knew about House Redcrest and if I had any allegiances there." Leoma shrugged. "But I don't know how I would when I'm not allowed to speak to anyone," she grumbled. "Then Ryden asked me if I was excited about my upcoming pairing and we talked about that for a bit."

Ana chewed her lip thoughtfully. "I don't understand why they would be asking that, especially out of the blue." She squinted at Leoma. "Have you been paired yet?"

"That is what I'm preparing for," she said. "It's going to be announced in the next few weeks—I think they were just trying to help prepare me. At least, that's what Heloise said." She shook her head and sighed. "I fear I may have made a fool out of myself with Duke Ryden, though. He's extremely handsome." She leaned forward, dropping her voice to a whisper. "I don't know how you're able to even think around him. He's the perfect Alpha!"

Ana smiled at her, but a dull gloom sobered her mood. This was exactly how Ana came across to others; innocent, ignorant, and gullible. Leoma was so sweet, but she didn't know much. She didn't even realize that her aunt and Ryden being together was unusual. Ana wouldn't have thought so a week ago either, but it clearly was. Why did everyone treat Omegas this way? She pushed the thoughts out of her mind. "It *is* exciting when you know you're about to be paired," she admitted.

"It is!" Leoma said, grinning wide. "I hope it's someone as nice as Ryden."

Ana patted her hand. "I'm sure it will be." She rose from his seat. "Thank you for seeing me, Leoma. It's been lovely to talk to you again."

Leoma blushed. "Thank you, Your Majesty. I am honored."

❖

Multiple thoughts dominated Ana's mind on the journey back to Ryden's mansion. Ryden seem to sense her thoughtfulness because he didn't try to engage in any kind of discussion or physical touching like he had on the way there. Ana was relieved about that because she was too tired to pretend.

Dusk had come and gone while they were at Sterling, and the velvety sky was streaked with the fading scores of lingering sun that somehow made her think of her nights with Maddoc. Immediately she pushed him out of her mind.

"You look tired, Ana," Ryden said, his voice low. "I hope you haven't been exhausted by today's visits."

Ana shook her head. "I will be capable of being married to you tomorrow, Ryden."

He didn't respond for a long moment. "This will be difficult for a while, Ana," he said. "But you will eventually come to terms with what is being asked of you."

"Don't you mean what is being asked of our children?"

"Ana," he growled. Something about the way he said it reminded her of Maddoc, and surprisingly her core clenched.

Ana stilled at the feeling. Was that a reaction to Ryden? Or the memory of Maddoc? She stared up at the sky, remembering two nights ago and his eagerness to fuck her as soon as he entered the room. She didn't even recall seeing the night sky while in that room with him; she'd never had the chance, even when he had her bent over the window—

"What are you thinking about?"

Ryden's voice brought her back to the smoothing jerking motion of the carriage. She swallowed, tucking the illicit thoughts away. There were more important things to discuss. "Why did you visit Leoma a couple of days ago?" she asked calmly.

In the semidarkness, she wasn't able to determine his expression, but something subtly changed in his posture. "Who told you that?"

"Does it matter?" Ana asked.

"Yes, it does." Ryden said irritably. "I don't want rumors spreading that I, a Redcrest duke, casually visits members of House Sterling. It will cause problems."

"You say that as though it's not true, like gossip to be discarded."

"I never said that."

"Then why even bother argue about it. If you don't want such rumors to spread, then don't do it."

Ryden growled again. "We talked about your tone with me, Ana."

Ana said, leaning forward and seeking out his eyes in the darkness, "I will treat you with the utmost respect that any Omega can give an Alpha, Ryden. I will be the perfect Omega and honor you for the rest of my life. But not if you lie to me. There is never any reason for an Alpha to lie to his Omega, is there?"

In the darkness, the tension in Ryden's body relaxed. "No," he said. "That is not the kind of relationship I wish to have."

"Then explain it to me. Are we at odds with Sterling, or not?"

"We are," Ryden said, his voice low. "I was visiting the houses to find a solution to our outlaw problem, and it made sense to visit House Sterling to see if there was a possibility of us coming to some kind of truce. Obviously it didn't work. Sterling is extremely aggressive in the way they deal with every other house. Leoma just happened to be there and Heloise invited me to visit with her. I think she thought she could use her to distract me so I would tell her what we were planning."

Ana pressed her lips together. That sounded like Heloise.

"I didn't mean to be defensive about it," he added. "I was just unprepared for your question. A lot of effort was made to ensure no one was aware of the meeting, beyond me and the person I met with. Unless Heloise told you, there is a security issue."

Ana sighed. "No, it was Leoma who told me. I don't think she realized she wasn't supposed to talk about it. She was excited to meet you."

"I'll send a message to ensure she knows not to talk about it. It was during quiet visits like that that I formed the alliance with Goldfrost and Thorneshaw. If everyone talked about them, we wouldn't have an alliance."

Ana nodded and leaned back against the carriage wall, the gentle jolting of its movement along the road rocking her. Secrets upon secrets. This was clearly the way of life as a royal, but she didn't like it, especially if it caused her to question her true mate. Maybe it was a silly thing to think, another remnant from the innocence that she had been steeped into for so long, but she had never seen any such deception between her parents. All she wanted was what they had. Granted, she didn't see them every single moment of every single day, but she'd been witness to their relationship her whole life, even during some of their private talks. She knew they had disagreements, but never any arguments or suspicions that would cause them to pull away from each other. She wondered if, at the beginning of their relationship, they had had any experiences like what she was having with Ryden. It would be helpful to ask them, but even if she could, she wouldn't know if they were telling her the truth. There was something strange about the way they lied about the Alpha and Omega stories. If the Atara in the books was not her mother, why would she be so keen to hide them?

Ana hadn't taken the time to fully think about it because so much had happened. And now she had left her home, Milly, her library, and all of her favorite books, including the Alpha and Omega stories that she only just discovered and had been looking forward to reading. Maybe they would give her answers about her lack of feeling for Ryden.

"Is there a way to collect anything from the palace?" she asked Ryden.

"Such as clothes?"

"No, belongings. I need some books from the library."

Ryden shook his head. "If it's an emergency, we will find a way to get it for you, but books can wait. After our wedding you will be moving back to the palace at some point, so you may not need to take them at all."

"What about Milly?"

Ryden frowned. "Who is that?"

"My lady-in-waiting."

He shook his head. "I'm sorry, Ana, but we can't use your father's staff. You can select a new lady-in-waiting as soon as things are settled."

Ana bit back the words she wanted to say, trying to ignore his implication that Milly was untrustworthy. Milly was the only one who'd been honest with her, and if she truly couldn't have Milly as her lady-in-waiting anymore, what would happen to her? Her status had already lowered from the death of her husband; her high-status job at the palace was the only thing keeping her afloat. Ana had said she would do whatever she could to help her, but now she couldn't.

But Ryden's words did highlight a fact she couldn't ignore; the palace was no longer her home, and no matter how much she might think of it as such, she would never be stepping back into it with the same status she had when she left.

Ana had always thought she would embrace change. Less than a week ago she had been looking forward to marriage and all the challenges and changes it would bring. But now the thought left her with a sick feeling in her stomach, and she couldn't pinpoint the reasons why. Her head had an understanding of how things were supposed to be, but her heart and her body had different ideas that conflicted with everything else, especially after her experiences with Maddoc. She would simply have to go to the library when she returned to find out what was wrong with her feelings for her mate.

For a moment she considered asking Ryden directly, but how would anyone start that kind of conversation? She would be effectively telling him that he wasn't as attractive to her as Maddoc, since the outlaw was her only comparison.

Ana gritted her teeth as she looked at the window, annoyed at how much Maddoc was still affecting her. She wished she'd never seen him or knew about him, but the memory of him entering the room, his overbearing smugness, and the way in which he handled her body and slipped inside her, telling her how hard she made him, caused such a deep tingle in her stomach that spread along her body until her aching nipples tingled yet again and she was wet between her legs.

"I hope you don't mind, but your wedding dress has been picked for you," Ryden said. "It should be at the mansion when we get back."

Ana nodded, keeping her face toward the window to avoid looking at him, as the shame of her instant arousal for the man she hated made tears come to her eyes. "That is fine," she said quietly.

FOUR

ANA

Ana stood in front of the mirror staring at her reflection. The handmaids from Ryden's mansion had done a good job. Not as good as Milly, of course, but at least nothing clashed with the color of her hair.

Tiny gems sewn into the deep emerald wedding gown shone and sparkled with every move she made. The style bared her shoulders, and the long sleeves elegantly tapered and sloped in a style that was highly fashionable in court. The tight corset accentuated her curves, while the skirt puffed out in multiple layers down to the floor. A beautiful train with a lace edge, at least four feet long, spread out behind her in an oval shape. Her crown had been collected from the palace and nestled onto her head. It'd taken two hours to arrange her red-copper locks into a delicate and elaborate hairstyle, showcasing her crown.

In the mirror she looked like a princess on her wedding day, but the confusion and revelations of the last few days dampened her elation and excitement.

This was all wrong.

"Are you ready, Your Majesty?" one of the handmaids asked.

Ana took a deep breath. "As ready as I'm going to be."

The handmaids helped her exit the door where the flower girls were waiting. As Ana turned into the corridor, they positioned themselves either side of her long train.

Since arriving at the Royal Sanctum, the ceremonial building where all royals married, Ana had practiced the route from her room to the altar twice. Ryden had stationed numerous knights along her route, as well as some knights to walk alongside her, which was a fair precaution, but all it did was add further strangeness to the day.

Usually when Ana had visited the venue, the serenity of the place settled her mind and uplifted her heart with a hopeful and romantic mood. Behind the main building was a beautiful garden, and situated at the end of it was the altar, an open structure where couples exchanged their vows. The walk through the gardens signified the shedding of one's old life and the embracing the rigor and beauty of a royal life together. It was a sacred place to wed, and Ana had been looking forward to her wedding day for years; the day she would finally echo the marital vows of her ancestors and every queen who had come before her. But the venue had lost some of its magic. Maybe it was the knights who surrounded her, maybe it was her lingering concerns about Ryden, or maybe the absence of her parents weighed heavily on her. Either way, the idyllic beauty she'd imagined for her day wasn't there.

However, as Ana reached to the top of the stairs where she would begin her walk to the altar, it was hard not to be in awe of the sight of the grounds before her. The altar's legendary gardens spread out, vast and luscious in its abundance, color and greenery. Tables and chairs set with satin emerald and white lace were decorated with flowers. The tables dotted the main area where the invited guests were waiting. A private woodland bracketed the gardens on one side, and on the other was a public viewing area where the Allandis people had gathered to watch, cheering when they saw Ana. Next to the altar, an orchestra played, the melodious strings soaring through the air and finally tugging on her spirits.

Ryden had already made his walk and stood under the thick archway decorated with flowers. She could just about make out his smile as he looked back at her.

At her entrance, the orchestra's music faded and the white-robed herald at the bottom of the stairs cleared his throat. "His and Her Majesties, royal houses, Lords and Ladies, give way for our royal bride, her Majesty, Princess Analisa of Allandis."

Guests from the royal houses and high society all looked upon her expectantly as the orchestra struck up again. Ana took a breath to steady her nerves. This was the most iconic part of all royal weddings—the bride's walk across the gardens. All she had to do was make her way down the steps, through the guests, and to the altar—the guests had even parted to make an aisle for her.

Ana began to descend down the steps keeping her head high. She took in the beauty of the sights before her and tried to draw upon the excitement of the event and ignore the signs that things weren't perfect—such as the large number of knights positioned around the edges of the gardens or that the most important people in her life were not there. Milly wasn't among the guests smiling in encouragement, Mother wasn't standing at the edge of the altar in her favorite ceremonial dress, and Father was not waiting at the foot of the stairs, waiting to assist her along the aisle.

Ana swallowed hard, pushing back the lump in her throat, and kept her eyes on Ryden, reminding herself that this was her true ascension into adulthood. She reached the bottom of the stairs and forced herself to relax as she began her walk.

A series of loud whips followed by muffled puncture sounds disoriented her. Then, all at once, every escorting knight around her fell to the ground, each with an arrow protruding from their chests. Ana froze—a silent horror building as their bodies twitched and jerked. When the flower girls began screaming, the shrill jolted her out of her stupor. Her head snapped up to Ryden, but he was too far away. Around the gardens, knights stumbled, as if attacked by some invisible force, and many dropped down like her guards had.

The guests realized what was happening and their voices rose in alarm as they began to run for shelter. The orchestra stopped playing abruptly, and the din from the crowd of commoners rose.

Ana couldn't help but scream at the horror of the dead bodies that surrounded her. Limp and crooked, some with open mouths of horror or surprise. The Alphas on the ground were men who were supposed to protect her, and terror gripped her at the idea she was so exposed and vulnerable.

She looked around frantically, trying to determine where the arrows were coming from or who was attacking them, but strange men suddenly appeared in the gardens. Huge, bulky Alphas dressed in layers of brown and grey, gripped swords or daggers. Each wore a black cloak with a hood that whipped around them as they attacked the remaining knights. Ana's heart jumped into her throat. Their black cloaks were almost the same as Maddoc's red one.

He was here.

Grabbing her skirts, she ran toward the altar. All she needed to do was get to Ryden and he would protect her—he'd said he could. She could see him looking at the guests and yelling but couldn't hear what he was saying. Just as his eyes landed on her, and relief softened his face, his whole right side jerked backward and he stumbled before falling to his knees, a thick arrow protruding from his shoulder.

Ana screamed, her fear blooming so quickly it overwhelmed her. *No!* Ryden couldn't be shot. She ran harder to get to him, but the guests scattered across the gardens blocking and obscuring her way as they tried to head to an exit.

A bellowing roar of multiple voices filled the air and the crowd slowed in confusion, giving her a chance to see an army of royal knights charge into the gardens from nearly every angle. She almost cried with relief at the sight of the royal insignia on their chests and the flag that rippled above their heads. Her father was here too! A sudden urge to find her father cut through her fear. No matter what happened between them, he would protect her, but she couldn't leave Ryden.

The quickening swish and clash of metal, deep grunts and yells signaled that the gardens had turned into a battleground and screeches filled her ears as the crowd became wilder in their attempt to get away, but she pushed forward unsure if she was still looking for Ryden or seeking out the protection of her father. She wasn't even sure where she was in the gardens anymore, but when a man stepped in front of her, parting the crowd like a rock in a creek, her whole body jolted, her horror turning into pure terror.

Maddoc stood staring at her with those hard, soulless eyes she'd seen when he first entered their room; only this time, the intense anger in them made her mouth dry. That familiar shiver and tremble burst into existence, and she edged backward, words frozen on her tongue.

He strode toward her, their eyes locked as though nothing else existed—as though no men fought and died around them, as though no arrows whipped by their heads. He wore the same layered clothes as before, complete with his red hood, but armor covered his chest and legs and the end of an enormous bow peeked over one of his shoulders. Within moments, he'd closed the gap between them, and as she turned—too late to escape—he swept her up with one arm, her back flush against his chest.

Maddoc turned and strode toward the woodlands on one side of the gardens, calm and relaxed as though he simply came to collect one of his belongings.

Ana held her breath, multiple raw and conflicting thoughts and emotions battering her insides as her mind tried to make sense of what was happening. Behind Maddoc, a battle was being waged in the gardens, every inch of it was filled with men fighting, and a nauseous wave rose to her throat. All this death and destruction. Wherever Maddoc went, this was what happened.

She wriggled in his grip, trying to fight her way out of his hold, but he pressed her tighter against him.

"You will not escape me again, Analisa." His coarse voice was loud in her ear. "Do not even try."

Just as she was about to respond, Maddoc abruptly stopped, his body jerking as the clang of swords rang out behind her.

Ana wriggled out of his grip as he fought, until she was able to slip from his arm, but he grabbed onto her and yanked her behind him as he continued to fight. The king's guard surrounded Maddoc in a close semicircle, engaging him in sword combat but unable to get close enough to her to pull her away from him. Even with one hand, he managed to hold off the kings most trained guards while he held onto her tight.

Looking around for a way to escape, Ana's heart rose at the sight of her father on horseback, his royal robe streaming behind him, his face grim and determined. He angled his horse toward her and leaned over to one side, his gaze trained on her. Ana's eyes widened, instinctively knowing what he intended to do. She widened her stance and bent her knees slightly, her heart pounding as Father neared.

The ground trembled as he approached, and as he passed Ana, he leaned over and grabbed her, wrenching her from Maddoc's grip and using the momentum of his body and her push off the ground to flip her behind him on the horse. Ana tried to find something to cling to in order to maintain her balance, but she was facing the wrong direction and the copious layers of material on her dress were not suited to remain upright on a saddle.

A thunderous roar tore through the air, and Ana held onto her seat as her eyes met Maddoc's. She wanted to look away, to avoid being targeted with his fury, but she'd never been able to. Tearing his eyes away from her, he threw his whole body into fighting even more furiously against the king's guard, his sword moving at lightning speed as he dispatched of her father's most skilled men. As soon as he speared the last one, his bow was in his hands and an arrow was already flying toward her before he'd barely looked up.

Ana didn't have time to scream. The arrow zipped past her and she heard a grunt behind her, followed by a low gurgling groan. *No!* Dread froze her heart as her father's horse began to slow.

"Father?" Ana tried to turn, but she was already trying not to slide off the horse. When her father leaned to one side, his hold on her slipped away, she dropped off the horse and to the ground, a hard jolt shuddering up her hip. "Father!" The commotion of the gardens swallowed her scream, but as she struggled with her dress to get to her feet, shouts of alarm caught her attention.

A few knights of the king's guard surrounded her father's horse, bringing it to a stop, but Ana's whole body turned cold when she saw her father, leaning to one side as the guards pulled him from his steed.

The arrow had shot him straight through his neck.

His guards lay him down on one side, some kneeling down to tend to him, others yelling across the gardens, but Ana couldn't remove her eyes from him, her horror and panic mounting. The arrow was lodged firmly through his neck and blood poured from the wounds, drenching his armor.

Ana headed toward him, tears stinging her nose as he writhed and clawed at his neck, his mouth opening and closing under his wide eyes. There was no way he could survive such a wound. He was going to die. "Father!" She began to run, but before she'd taken even two steps toward him, a thick arm lifted her off the ground and she was once again against the outlaw's chest.

He turned away from the gardens, this time running toward the woodland.

"Father!" Ana screamed so loud her throat burned, and she fought Maddoc with everything she had, trying to twist out of his grip and get back to the gardens, but the Alpha wrapped both of his thick, heavy arms around her torso this time, securing her against his chest.

"Let me go!" She punched Maddoc's arms and dug her fingers into the massive muscles trying to pry him off her. "Father!" She craned her head to look back at the gardens but within moments, her father was no longer in view. The Alpha weaved through the trees surprisingly nimbly, his hold tight, and the cries and commotion from the gardens faded the farther they went.

"Maddoc, put me down!"

He didn't answer, his breathing steady and heavy as he trudged through the trees.

But the image of her father bleeding on the ground burned into Ana's mind, fanning the flames of her panic and fear for his life. Using every ounce of energy she could, she fought against his hold, kicking, screaming, punching, twisting, and straining against every part of the Alpha that touched her. She couldn't leave her father like that. She just couldn't. He was most certainly dying and she wouldn't keep quiet or be a good little Omega when her father, who tried to save her from this man, lay bleeding to death in the gardens where her wedding was to take place.

Fresh tears filled her eyes and the more she thought of her father, the man she'd always looked up to, the man who raised her, the more the dread overwhelmed her. She would never see him again. The sobs came so deeply that she could barely breathe, but she still fought, struggling to be released from the bastard who had started all of this, intending to ruin her, and now he had killed her father. She fought him with everything she had, until she was so hysterical that he was unable to hold her.

He abruptly halted, allowing her to slip from his arms, but holding onto her upper arms with both hands. "You'd better fucking behave, Analisa!"

"No!" She wrenched herself from him so hard, pain ricocheted up her arms. "I want to see my father. He is bleeding to death back there!"

"He knew the risks coming here today." The anger in his bellowing tone roared through her. "He shouldn't have taken you from my arms after I had already obtained you. It is the height of his dishonor to try and take what has already been claimed by someone else—"

"I don't give a fuck about your honor!" Ana screamed, her throat burning with each word released. "You said you wouldn't kill him."

"What did you expect, Ana?" The growling agitation in his tone made his words even more threatening. "What did you think would happen when you *disobeyed* me?" The darkness in his eyes reached a ferocity that made her shiver. "I told you no one should touch you, or everyone you care about would die. And instead of abiding by that rule, you ran away to get fucking married!" He stepped forward and grabbed her neck, roughly yanking her toward him, the acrid scent of his fury stifling her. "And you let him *touch* you."

Ana's own fury was fed by his. "He is my—"

"He is *nothing*," the Alpha roared. "He has no right to touch what is mine!" He stepped forward, forcing her to step back. "What exactly did you do with him in his mansion?"

Ana glared at him, unable to believe that this was the height of his concern while her father lay bleeding to death. But then what did she expect? He was the one who had fatally wounded him. Ana firmed her mind and tilted up her chin. She would not bend to this man—this murderer—anymore. "Take me back to—"

"Answer me!" he roared, pushing her back farther and forcing her to retreat. "Did you fuck him?"

"I want to see my father!"

The Alpha pushed her back harder until her back slammed against a rough tree bark, it's uneven gnarly knobs ramming into her back. She forced herself not to cry out.

"You will never see your father again if you do not answer me!" the Alpha roared.

Ana glared up at him, the anger between them thick and suffocating, but in that moment, she saw what she was really looking at. This man was a monster. The darkest black fury consumed him, bulging at his neck, darkening his eyes, clenching his huge muscles. His whole body was poised to attack, and every sense within her told her that he was bordering on the edge of control. The worst was the pungent scent seeping from him, entrenched with his aggression, flared an intense longing in the pit of her stomach, bringing with it a twisted admiration and desire at the sight and smell of an Alpha with such intensity and violence. Ana grit her teeth, willing the feeling away. "No, I did not fuck him."

The Alpha's stance did not change. "Did he touch you?"

Ana's mouth tightened. "Not... like that."

"Then how?"

Ana held his violent gaze. "Please take me back to my father."

The Alpha pulled her forward until his lips almost touched hers, then he slammed her back on the gnarly bark. This time a biting pain dug into her back, and she had to cry out. "How?" he demanded.

Ana gasped, blinking rapidly as tears stung her eyes from the pain. "He… kissed me. That's all."

All bravery deserted Ana when an enraged roar erupted from the Alpha; the roar so violent it shook the trees around them. His mouth slammed against hers, knocking her head onto the tree bark, and he kissed her so hard, it hurt.

She pushed back against his thick shoulders, trying to pull her mouth away, but it didn't make a difference. He bit and sucked on her lips and pushed his tongue into her mouth, punishing and brutal. Ana tried to bite him, to be just as violent in response, but it seemed as though he didn't even feel her resistance. As their mouths battled, his scent deepened into that familiar rich complexity tainted by the harshness of aggression, and Ana's desire flared in response, just as violently as his kiss. Her nipples grew so taut, they stung with that rushing sensation she'd relished back in their room, accompanied by an exquisite throbbing between her legs.

Horrified, she wrenched her head away, panting hard. Father had to be taking his last breath by now, if he was even alive at all, and she was becoming dangerously aroused by this bastard. "Maddoc." She didn't like the way her voice trembled. "Let me—"

The Alpha released her neck, gripped the skirts of her dress and tore them down the middle.

"What are you doing?" Ana gasped.

She wasn't sure if the Alpha heard her. His hand dipped to her thighs, digging into them as he pried them open.

Ana's fury surged again. Raising a hand, she slapped him across the face as hard as she could, the crack of her hand echoing through the trees.

It fucking hurt her hand, but Maddoc's head barely moved. Annoyingly, the violence in his eyes changed to a hot smolder, and Ana's own craving peaked to a tortuous need. Her whole body was aflame at the way he was looking at her, coupled with his scent, and she remembered—he liked when she slapped him—or at least when she was angry enough to do so. "Don't touch me," she spat, a sob almost escaping that she couldn't control the conflict within her. "You are letting my father die without me. Don't ever touch me again."

"I don't give a fuck what you want." Maddoc's growl was so low, it vibrated through her chest. "You have been irresponsible with this body, even after all my warnings."

"Stop trying to make this about me!" Her voice sounded shrill in her ears but she didn't care. "All you want to do is turn this entire kingdom to chaos and upend the royal structure. You want everyone to be at the mercy of you and your men. I want no part of it."

"It has always been about you." Maddoc hooked his hand under her thigh and lifted her leg. "You have no choice, Princess. "

"Yes, that's right," she remarked bitterly. "Everyone has to suffer for the actions of other people, just like making me suffer because of my father."

"Do not act like you didn't beg me to fuck you," Maddoc said dangerously, his other hand releasing himself from his pants, "or knot you or suck that clit until you screamed. You wanted everything I gave you. The only time you didn't reach for my cock was when you were asleep. Do not act like it was any *hardship* for you!"

Ana glared at him, forcing herself not to lower her eyes, even though the embarrassment at his truthful words coursing through her was almost unbearable.

Maddoc lowered his face until his mouth was against hers, his black eyes staring directly at her. "And do not act like you are not wet right now, needing me to fuck this aggression out of you. Don't act like your pussy isn't sopping and twitching and waiting for me, because I can smell it."

With that, he drove into her in one single spearing thrust, and Ana wailed in relief as the burn she needed rocketed up her core, flaring an erotic rejoicing throughout her body that made every hair on her arms and neck stand on end. It was though her body celebrated the feel of him inside her again, and she clung to him, knowing she needed it. He slammed so deep inside her she gasped, pumping a rhythm that slapped her hips against the tree bark as he worked in and out. His lips remained on hers, grunting into her mouth as he claimed every moan and whimper that escaped it. As her body jolted against the knobby bark, searing pains rocked into her back, worsening with each slam, and yet it fed into the bitter sweetness of the savage rapture that had overtaken her. All thoughts were shunted out of her mind as her body tuned in to the deliciously overwhelming sensations coursing through her.

"So good," he grunted into her mouth before biting her bottom lip.

Ana agreed but couldn't speak.

She was so wet, her slick spurted out of her, as he worked in and out, dripping along her thighs. She found herself annoyed that his skin was partially obscured by their clothing, but he yanked her neckline down and encircled her hard nipples, and suddenly she was mindless with pleasure. When her orgasm came, it was with the violence of both of their fury, and it wrecked her completely. Tearing through every muscle in her body and sweeping away whatever resolve she had left. By the time the Alpha's release neared, Ana was limp, her body battering against the tree bark as it bruised her spine, her head limp to one side.

The Alpha withdrew and pushed Ana to her knees as he spurted his seed all over her. The warmth splashed her face and neck, and in the mindless numbness of it, Ana reveled in the satisfaction of his mark on her and the rawness between her legs. But slowly, as the Alpha continued to mark her, her mind began to clear. The gritty scent the of soil underneath her knees rushed into her nose bringing her back to her surroundings. At the Alpha's last grunt, she noticed cloaked men standing farther back in a semicircle in the woodlands, their backs to them. They were his men.

Instantly, the image of her father sprang back to her mind and tears welled in her eyes, a dark gloom growing in her chest.

After fixing his pants, Maddoc yanked Ana up by her elbow and lifted her again into his arms, striding through the woodlands without saying a word.

Ana barely had the strength to fight him anymore, but she saw he was not heading back toward the gardens—he was heading away from it.

"Wait," she croaked, her throat sore. "You said you would let me see my father."

The Alpha said nothing.

Too tired to say anything more, Ana remained limp in his arms, nursing a bitter sorrow. He'd lied. He told her what she wanted to hear and then fucked her knowing she wouldn't see her father again.

They arrived at a clearing where a group of men and women waited atop horses, along with an enormous black horse that had no rider. Maddoc placed Ana sideways in the saddle and swung up behind her. Nodding at his people, Maddoc spurred the horse into action, and led them through the woodland with Ana leaning against his chest.

The dissolution in her heart made her numb. Her father was dead and her true mate was likely dead too. She would probably never know the extent of what happened at her wedding, how many of her father's knights survived, or even if any of the guests were hurt. What she did know was that without the king, the kingdom was certain to descend into chaos and that must have been what Maddoc wanted all along. He may have acted like he was angry with her for leaving, but this had to be the perfect result for him. No king on the throne meant the opportunity for anarchy.

She gritted her teeth as she closed her eyes, relishing the bitterness between her legs and the sharp ache in her back. Pain roared around her body almost as unbearable as the pain in her heart, but she welcomed it. It echoed the ferocity of her anger—anger that she was still so attracted to him, anger that her mother would be without her true mate, and anger that the kingdom had lost a truly great monarch.

But at least Maddoc had shown his true colors beyond any shadow of doubt. He had killed her father and then fucked her against a tree while she begged to see him. There was nothing about this man's brutality that had been untrue, as much as he may want to play with words to make it seem so.

She forced the sobs in her throat down as hard as she could as the clarity of her situation revealed itself to her. She was his property now, but that didn't mean she had to willingly take whatever he gave to her. Granted, her body may be lost to her at times, but he did not need or deserve anything else. So she made a vow in honor of her father's memory, in honor of her mother, in honor of Milly and Ryden, that she would never stop fighting him, that she would never make it easy for him, and that she would take her last breath before she gave or asked him for anything ever again. He may take her body, but he would never take her sanity or her mind, her love or her loyalty for those whom he made suffer. The first thing he would never have was her purr, the second was her words.

From the moment she had argued with him, he had taken to pacifying her with lies or ignoring her completely. So just like Milly suggested that first night, she would not speak to him. The man thrived on seeing her upset, on hearing her beg him, on the anger in her words. But he would not get that anymore.

If Maddoc wanted the Omega princess, the heir of the kingdom, he could have her. But he would get an empty shell. That was all he deserved.

FIVE

MADDOC

Maddoc maintained a tight grip on Analisa as they rode through the woodlands and across the outer farming fields toward the Oakenshire Forest.

Anger still roiled in his gut, but it was tempered by a mellow satisfaction that he finally had her with him. She'd been subdued since beginning the journey, but that was expected. He had been rough with her, but Analisa had to learn what would happen when lines were crossed, and while he might enjoy her willfulness, he at no point would ever enjoy the idea of another man having his mouth on her. Claiming and marking her against the tree had been an instinctual need for both of them, and her denial to see or accept the way her body reacted to him—or that she was his—was no excuse for her behavior. Now he had her, she would have to adjust to her new life and accept the truths before her, whether she liked them or not.

The riding party angled toward the central city, skimming the edge of the orchards maintained for the royals before veering back out again toward the larger districts that bordered the largest and wildest natural forest in the kingdom, the Oakenshire.

They entered at a full gallop, a sense of urgency uniting the riders as they headed back to their base deep within the forest. Much had happened at the wedding, some of which Maddoc didn't expect, but the ultimate goal had been achieved. His Omega was in his arms, and she would not escape again.

"I'll set up some surveillance for the night," Griff called.

Maddoc raised his hand to signal that he agreed, and three of the men broke away and rode in a different direction.

They traveled on for a while, having to slow as the forest grew dense with trees. When it was too thick to ride through, they dismounted and one of the men led the horses back the way they'd come. The base was only accessible by navigating through some of the thickest parts of the forest, and although they had cut enough of it back to walk through, it was too uneven and thick for the horses.

Maddoc carried Analisa in his arms. She curled herself up in her torn dress and said nothing to him, her head tucked down to her chin. He allowed her her peace. She would be required to face him soon enough, but for now he allowed her to mourn her father.

The skies were dark by the time they trudged into the base, an enormous clearing filled with huts, tents, and structures that made up the center of operations for the guild. When he selected this site, he'd made sure it was completely secure. Thick forest surrounded almost the whole area, and the

Oakenshire was so large it could house the entire base comfortably without anyone being able to find it unless they knew the location. The clearing was so far from anything notable within the forest, it was likely anyone trying to leave would get lost and never be seen again. As such, Maddoc had always felt safe here, as did the people who joined him.

Maddoc made his way straight to his pavilion. The base was mostly quiet that night, with only the fading campfires of those preparing for sleep.

He headed toward the most secluded part of the base, and as he neared his pavilion, Raine approached him.

"What?" he bit out the word irritably.

She hesitated, eyeing Ana. "It can wait. There is nothing we can do until morning anyway."

"Good," Maddoc said, walking past her.

His pavilion was one of the most lavish. It was an elaborate tent-like structure with multiple rooms built on a solid frame, including its own washroom situated next to a well with a pump. Maddoc placed Ana down on his bed and tore her dress off, ignoring her flinch from the roughness of the act. When he'd watched her approach the stairs at the Royal Sanctum through his magnifying lens, he knew at that moment he was going to rip this dress apart. Everything it signified infuriated him.

He drew a bath, then lifted her and placed her into the water before undressing.

Ana didn't look at him once, keeping her eyes averted as he climbed into the bath with her. The hot water did nothing to soothe his mood, but Ana relaxed a little, sighing as she closed her eyes and sunk deeper into the water.

Without saying anything, he soaped her up, scrubbing her skin and eliminating all traces of anything and anyone else. Of course, he couldn't prevent himself from becoming aroused by her. His woman's body was phenomenal, and just the sight of her pert nipples made his mouth water. On a whim, he drew her into his lap and tucked his nose into her neck, breathing in the scent that he would always kill for. As he inhaled, he finally began to relax a little.

He ran his nose behind her ear and then down along her jaw until his mouth reached hers, and then he kissed her, pulling her closer to him, his hand lowering to the middle of her shoulders as he claimed her pretty, succulent mouth the way he loved.

Immediately, the princess winced.

He pulled back slowly, watching her. "What is it, Analisa?"

She kept her eyes averted and didn't say a word.

Maddoc growled in displeasure but reminded himself that she was still grieving. He pressed the back of her shoulders again and watched her carefully as his hand lowered down her back. She winced again, her body jerking as pain flashed across her face.

Maddoc twisted her around and was shocked to see bruises and gashes on her back.

"When did this happen?" Maddoc demanded, turning her back around.

Ana did not answer. Keeping her gaze away, she firmly ignored him.

"Analisa, when did this happen to your back?"

She didn't answer again, and this time he noticed her jaw was hard, her teeth were clenched. He growled in annoyance, she was refusing to answer him.

He thought back to the events of the day, trying to figure out when she got hurt. He'd kept a close eye on her the whole time she had traveled to the altar, and then as soon as she appeared at the top of the steps, and began to walk, he had kept his eyes on her constantly. There was no other time for her to be damaged unless it was when she was getting ready, and she didn't look as though she walked in pain.

"Tell me, Analisa," he murmured, slipping his hand between her legs. "Tell me how you were hurt."

Ana said nothing, didn't even respond to his hand, although her breath hitched when he touched her.

Maddoc couldn't help but smile. Ana always reacted beautifully to him, no matter how much she might want to deny it. Even when she was begging to see her father, she was so aroused by his presence, just as he was by hers.

He froze, remembering their rough coupling in the woods. He had thrown her against the tree.

He cursed loud and hard, his mood souring that he was the one who had damaged her.

"Why didn't you tell me you're hurt," he bellowed, forcing her around again to look at the injury. It had to hurt.

Ana said nothing.

Maddoc finished washing them both, carefully cleaning Ana's back, before climbing out of the bath and carrying her to the bedroom. Grabbing a jar of healing salve from his dresser, he applied it gently.

"This will aid the healing. It may take a few days, but it will heal without any lingering bruises and scars."

Once again, she said nothing.

"Ana," Maddoc said warningly. "Your grief about your father is not a reason to ignore your injuries. If you are hurt, you do not ever hide that."

Ana kept her head down and remained still and silent.

"Analisa!" Maddoc grabbed her shoulders and yanked her to face him, but when her eyes landed on him he saw that she was not depressed or desolate at all. The fire in her eyes was just as strong, if not stronger than it had always been. And it was full of hate. She was *choosing* not to speak to him. Immediately Maddoc growled, grabbing the back of her head, and he rose up to kneel on the bed, leaning over her. "When I speak, you will respond."

The look in her eyes hardened and her mouth tightened as though she was resolving that she would never speak.

Annoyed, Maddoc let out a gruff growl and pulled at her hair, releasing all the pins and nets so her beautiful, red hair could fall free around her shoulders. "You think you can remain silent?" He hooked his arms under her legs and pulled her forward slightly, forcing her to drop back on her elbows, he then slapped her legs open, spreading them so far that her bare pussy tilted up at him. It was already shining, waiting for him, and as usual, his whole body responded. "Do you think you will last a day without screaming for me?"

Ana didn't move a muscle, didn’t try to close her legs or resist him. Instead, she averted her eyes to a spot behind him, as if removing herself from the situation in her mind, and removing her thoughts from him.

That was unacceptable!

Maddoc rumbled his displeasure and grabbed her breast, squeezed it hard as he dove down to her pussy. She inhaled sharply, but didn't make a sound as he pinched her nipple and wriggled his tongue along her slit.

Fuck, this woman always tasted so good. He wasn't sure how he'd managed to survive without her taste, her scent—it was simply magnificent. He lapped her pussy, dipping and stroking into every crevice and nibbling her juicy folds. Her potent, tangy slick oozed, sliding on his tongue and filling his nose so strongly, he moaned with pleasure. Ana's breathing deepened, and her pussy twitched. When he pressed his tongue into her, moving his hand to pinch her other nipple, she awarded him a moan, and he smiled as he latched onto her clit, suckling gently as he grabbed her ass, his need for her building.

By the time her clit was throbbing, Ana was crying out, writhing and shuddering on the bed as her climax gripped her in its beautiful crescendo—like it always did.

Maddoc rose up, then pushed straight into her, eager to be inside her again. Her pussy clenched around him and he groaned sinking deep to the root, his balls resting against her ass as she arched her back to accept him.

When he began to thrust, her pussy was so wet that each delicious sloppy slam echoed through the pavilion. Ana writhed underneath him, her breasts swaying and jiggling, her hips humping up to take him harder and deeper, and all he could do was watch her, mesmerized, as he had done for the entirety of the first two nights he was with her. In truth, Ana had surprised him more than he ever thought possible. It wasn't just her fiery response to him, or her willingness to fight back as hard as she did, but she blossomed sexually from the moment he ordered her to open her legs. Though she hummed and squealed with delight when he dominated her, she also wanted things her own way. She scolded him when he didn't listen, and was willing to fight back and claim the situation as her own. Even when she had slapped him for not listening, it had been refreshing to watch the so-called docile princess so flush with anger to be moved to violence in that way. It had been the most beautiful thing he had ever seen. And then when he'd actually taken her, she licked and arched, and sucked, and purred… needing his cock and seed in her mouth. She reveled in his body and in his scent, just as he did in hers, doing every instinctive thing he'd heard Omegas did but never quite believed. It was an unparalleled experience, one that he knew could never be replicated anywhere else.

No one else could have that from her, and he was satisfied knowing that no one had.

He increased his thrusts, shunting into her tight, undulating body, carnal pleasure and ecstasy forcing coarse grunts from his throat with each push of his hips and clench of his ass.

Whatever protest Ana was trying to make by not speaking to him could not last. Not the way she moaned and ground her hips. However, Maddoc noticed that her eyes were lidded. He grabbed her jaw and tilted her face to his, watching her expression of bliss as she climbed to another crescendo.

Her orgasms were always the most erotic thing about being with her. Her tense body, her breathy cry, and the gush of her slick—it was intoxicating.

Pounding harder, Maddoc increased his speed, clawing at her breasts as she screamed at her peak, his own climax approaching. As the rush of devastating pleasure exploded, a roar erupted from his throat and he jammed his knot into her swollen sheath, almost breathless at how tightly she encapsulated him.

Ana rotated her hips as he ground himself deep within her and he groaned, dropping over her small body and pushing her off her elbows and onto her back.

Their coarse, loud breaths saved the room from silence, and Maddoc closed his eyes, reveling in the ongoing pleasure his Omega was giving him; her panting body underneath him, her heels digging into his ass to keep him deep within her, the clench of her channel milking his spurting cock. He rumbled in satisfaction and tucked an arm underneath her, but it was only when she winced that he remembered her back. Rolling over onto his side, he pulled her to lie next to him, tucking his bicep under her head for her to rest on. Her eyes were closed, the expression on her face relaxed.

"You would never have been able to keep quiet for long," he said, his tone smug as he brushed her hair out of her face. "You are too vocal, Analisa. It is one of things I love about you."

But when her eyes opened to meet his, the hardness was still there and after a moment of glaring at him, she averted her eyes. Maddoc suddenly realized that she had moaned and screamed, but she hadn't said his name or formed any words at all.

"Analisa," he growled sharply. "You will speak!"

But no matter what he said, what threat he made, Analisa's mouth remained shut. As soon as his knot shrunk, he was pounding into her again, this time on her hands and knees as he pulled her head back and forced her back to arch, pushing her ass in the air. It was one of the most delicious positions, the roundness of her ass another mesmerizing sight as he battered into her, each slam rippling those perfect cheeks.

But Ana still did not speak.

The next time he had her against the pavilion floor, then on the table in the living area, and then he was so incensed by her silence that he filled her throat with his seed, roaring that if she wasn't making use of it, then he would.

Each time, regardless of however powerful her orgasm was, Analisa did not speak, not even one word. She barely even looked at him.

Maddoc fucked her all night, each time rougher than the last, each orgasm racking her body harder, until she was so exhausted she could barely move, and she fell asleep on his knot.

Maddoc played with her hair as he fumed. Clearly, she blamed him for not allowing her to see her father in his final moments, but what he had done was a kindness. She didn't realize that, but how could she? She barely knew anything that was going on around her. Still, he would not allow her to be disrespectful or disobedient.

He growled in annoyance as she slept, recognizing that this beauty was finally his, but yet he could not control her. It was fucking ironic considering the way she'd been controlled by everyone else. He couldn't start their three nights again while she was in this rebellious state; it wouldn't work.

So if she was choosing to be difficult, he would have to be drastic and break the silence out of her until she once again begged and pleaded for him.

❖

The next morning should have been blissful.

Maddoc woke with his Omega's scent in his nose, her soft body tucked into his, her dried slick all over his face and her gentle breathing in his ears. She was finally in his pavilion. It should have been perfect, except it wasn't.

Ana lie awake, her eyes on the ceiling, her breathing calm. Maddoc didn't even try to engage her. He rolled onto his back, pulling her on top of him and pulled her up so he could suck on her nipples. She kept herself limp and unresponsive, but the whimpers began when he gently bit her nipple and sucked it hard and twisted his mouth around it. Her head lolled to one side and her body twitched, her hips rotated, seeking the gratification he could give her, the savagery that she needed, but he didn't give it to her. Kissing up her neck, he scented her slowly, running his nose to the back of her ear and back down her neck, taking great pleasure in her scent and the way it settled him. It pulled on every instinct, singing and tugging on everything in him to own this woman. His cock jerked on his stomach, leaking as it sought to provide lubrication for what was to come.

Maddoc bit her ear, sucking the lobe and flicking his tongue along it, satisfied to hear the way she whimpered.

"You are exquisite, Analisa," he mumbled, almost to himself, as he sunk his nose back behind her ear. “I am glad you are finally here.” A sudden gust of her sweet intoxicating scent perfumed the air around them, signifying her need.

Maddoc’s cock hardened to the point of pain, but he lifted her off him and placed her next to him on the bed. “I will fuck you again when you choose to behave,” he said, glaring at her.

For the first time, various expressions flitted across Ana’s face, and Maddoc noted both surprise and smugness. “You think I have been forcing you to suffer on my cock.” He leaned forward and kissed her sticky slit before looking up at her. “If that is the case, you will not want me again. And I doubt that will ever be the case.”

The scowl that appeared on her face would have been humorous, if he wasn’t so furious about having to punish her this way. But he didn’t dwell on it, instead he briskly got up to get dressed. Her pussy tasted ripe for fucking, and if he didn’t go, he might break his rule immediately.

"You will not leave this pavilion," he instructed, as he dressed. "At least not until your back is healed."

Ana clenched her teeth as she glared at him. She turned away and laid down on the bed.

Maddoc growled his displeasure but didn't say anything more. Her punishment would be harder than she knew, and although he would suffer too, he would not accept her denial of their attraction anymore. Once she accepted that they belonged together, everything else would be manageable. So the next time they fucked, it would be because she begged for it, nothing less. And they had the rest of their lifetimes for that to happen, though he expected she wouldn't last until tomorrow.

He turned away from her and refocused his mind. Now that his Omega was safe in his pavilion and at his base, certain things needed addressing.

When he exited his pavilion, all of his commanders were gathered by the local campfire talking amongst themselves. They quietened when they saw him, all of their faces grave. Maddoc knew what it was about and beckoned them to the meeting tent.

Once they were seated at the table inside, he braced himself. "How bad is it?"

"Bad," Griff said bluntly. His second-in-command Alpha looked disheveled from being up all night, but his eyes were sharp. "Redcrest and Sterling are, of course, fighting for the crown, but they have all agreed that they must unite to retaliate."

Maddoc frowned. "How?"

"By coming for us."

"Coming here?" Maddoc asked. "What makes them think they will find us when they haven't before?"

"They intend to make a good effort of it," Walrick said gravely. "They are using all their own resources, the king's guard and… the people."

Maddoc tensed. "What do you mean, the people?"

"They are rounding up everyone who *might* have seen any of us or seen the direction we may have headed and are questioning them," Griff said. "Three families have already been killed… ones loyal to us."

"Fuck!" Maddoc stood abruptly, kicking back his chair in his outrage and pacing across the tent. He clenched his fists and turned back to the table, forcing himself to ask. "Who?"

"The Bennetts, the Haywards, and the Wrights."

Maddoc cursed again, his anger turning to fury. All of those families had young children—most of the families who supported Maddoc's cause did. And now they were all at risk.

"We have to go home, Doc," Bram said, though his voice was resigned. "We can't stay and risk 'em findin' us here. You have your woman. Let's go now while we have the chance."

"I gave my word to those families, Bram," Maddoc bellowed. "We cannot leave them."

"Then you shouldn't have shot the king." Raine's voice was quiet but firm.

The other commanders remained silent. Only Raine got away with pushing the boundaries by speaking to him like that, and she only did it when she felt there was a need. Maddoc still didn't like it.

"Where did they put him?" he asked.

"Back at the palace."

"Did Agnes go?"

Raine nodded. "I haven't heard from her."

It doesn't matter," another man, Percy, said. "This changes things. We never planned to assassinate the king. It will not bode well for us with the people, even those loyal to us. It will upset the balance too much."

"And we have the heir to the throne," Griff pointed out. "They have an incentive to attack us until they get her back."

"I'm not sure about that," Walrick said. "This is the chance for Sterling and Redcrest to take the throne."

"It's not that simple," Griff said. "There is no outside influence in this scenario. None of them will want to risk being usurped for taking the throne improperly. It is easier if they have the heir."

"Well, they're not going to get her," Maddoc thundered. "That should not be a surprise."

Griff shook his head. "No, but they will try hard to." He inhaled a breath. "I must agree with Bram, Maddoc. We have to go home sooner rather than later."

"No." Maddoc shook his head. "This just means we execute our plans early, all at the same time. We will still have success while the kingdom is in disarray, we just have to get it done quicker." He looked at all of his commanders. "I trust you will work to ensure that it gets done."

Each of the commanders nodded, except Bram. Bram was a slim man, unassuming in many ways, nothing remarkable about the way he looked, but for his strategic mind. He tilted his head at Maddoc. "If we don't leave now," he said slowly, "we risk never leaving at all. They will find us here, and they will be desperate to get her back. They will slaughter us and keep their actions hidden in this forest. The longer we stay, the more risk there is to everyone here."

Maddoc gritted his teeth, annoyed at Bram's assessment of the situation, but he couldn't ignore him, not when he relied on him so much for all of his strategic plans.

But Maddoc would not break his word to the people who had risked their lives to help him, to help them all, and he still had to open Ana's eyes to the truth of her precious court. If he didn't, she would never accept that what he'd done had been the best thing for them both.

Part of Maddoc wished he hadn't been so cryptic with her during their two nights together, that he'd been able to tell her everything. But she was too much of a puppet, and still was, and had been conditioned not to believe anything he said. That he'd had to get her in his arms through the Royal Promise was already enough of a disgrace, but the fact she didn't even recognize what there was between them, that she fought him at every turn, was testament to how far and how securely she'd been manipulated by her parents.

He walked back to the table. "It is the people out there in the kingdom who risk their lives, yet still help our cause, who are the bravest among us," he began. "They risk themselves and their families and their livelihoods every day—we would not have achieved anything without them. I will not abandon them. I cannot—it was *my* arrow in the king's neck yesterday. So all of you are welcome to leave now if you wish," he began. "I have never forced anyone to stay or to work on this goal with me against their wishes. The only one who is forced to be here is the princess. So if you want to go home, or go anywhere, go. Take any man or woman who wants to go with you and take the weapons you have built. See how you fare. You could survive better in the current circumstances." He leaned forward on the table, his hands planted firmly. "Just know that if you reveal anything about the guild, or our plans you will be killed as is protocol."

All of the commanders were already shaking their heads.

"I am not saying we *want* to leave," Bram clarified. "I'm saying we should, to avoid any possibility of being captured or killed."

"Plus some of the new highcloaks haven't finished their training," Griff said. "They're still learning our methods and ways. This is not the time for us to rely on new warriors."

"I agree," Maddoc said. "It should be awhile before they locate us. Finish the training of those who have already started but demote any who are not ready. If there is someone you wouldn't trust your life with, they must go." He looked at all of his commanders. "Is that clear?"

They all nodded.

"Good. Then we move on with our plan. Just one more thing," Maddoc said. "We have an Omega at our base now. This is hers as much as anyone else's, but she is an unwilling resident. I assume you remember the protocols we talked about being in place for when she is here."

All of the commanders nodded.

"Good. That must be enacted now and at all times. Another thing, none of the highcloaks are to talk to her."

There was a long silence. The commanders stared at him, a couple of them glanced at each other. "But we are all highcloaks… at least, in the active guild…."

"Exactly," Maddoc said. "Make sure all of them know."

The confusion on the commanders' face smoothed out, but he could tell they didn't understand the request. Fortunately, they didn't need to understand to carry it out. "Understood?"

They all nodded, and Maddoc pulled forward the maps and began pouring over everything and discussing their plans. He needed to be careful with everything he did from now on, and it didn't help that in the middle of this, Ana was being so difficult. He understood she blamed him, and that she was grieving, but he couldn't allow anything negative to fester between them.

But it didn't matter. He still had her, and once she realized the raw instinctual power of their attraction, her behavior would not last. Soon she would be begging for his cock, and his kisses, and to be by his side as his woman, where she belonged.

Six

ANA

Ana sunk deep into the bitterness of the gloom that smothered her.

Everything in her life had changed so drastically in the last day and she'd barely had time to think about it, but as soon as Maddoc left and her anger faded, she was alone with her thoughts, and the horror of everything that had happened weighed her down.

Father was dead.

It was unbelievable. He'd had a long reign ahead of him, and of all the things he could have died for, it shouldn't have been because he was trying to protect his daughter. She couldn't even imagine how distraught Mother would be. As his fated mate, she would likely never be the same again, and that kind of loss was devastating, not just for them, but for Ana who had watched them all her life. The thought darkened her mood, bringing fresh sobs to her chest and an overwhelming sense of loss, guilt, and shame.

This was her fault. She shouldn't have left the palace. If she'd stayed with her parents and spent the last night with Maddoc as planned, they would still be alive, and Father may have successfully killed the outlaw on the final morning. Instead, her parents and her fated mate were gone. And she was alone in a strange place with an unreasonable, violent Alpha.

She wasn't sure what would happen with the royal houses, especially with what she had learned about them recently. She could only hope they would take on the responsibilities the Kingdom of Allandis required of them. The people needed them more than ever—they couldn't let Maddoc win.

He'd been one step ahead of everyone from the beginning, and if she was going to survive him, she had to be smarter. Even if she never escaped him, she would not give him what he wanted. He seemed to want to keep her as a trophy, an ornament of the kingdom he toppled, the last remnant of the king he murdered. But she wouldn't allow him to do that.

Granted, she couldn't do anything about how easily her body reacted to him, how quickly she became aroused, or how eager she sought to have him inside her. He had ensured he'd be the first to fuck her, and he'd somehow tuned her body to his so she would find him intoxicating—his taste, his scent, the feel of him against her. The attraction was intense and addicting, and she was powerless against it. So she tried to push away all guilt and accept that this was her fate; to be his whore the way he'd always intended, after all, he had been right—it wasn't only three nights. But now she may even escape that duty. It was laughable he thought withholding sex was a punishment that would force her to talk to him. It was actually an incentive to never speak again! He could wait forever as far as she was concerned.

Regardless of being his prisoner, she couldn't abandon any of her beliefs or values just because she was forced to share his bed or live among criminals. She had to be true to herself and still be Princess Ana, but now, she could be the Ana she wanted to be, the Ana she needed to be to help her people in whatever way she could. And the first thing she needed to do was find out more information. She wouldn't take anyone's word for anything. It was time to take her own learning in hand.

Standing up, she took her time examining the different rooms of Maddoc's pavilion. It was built well; it was similar to one of the small cottages in the kingdom's villages, complete with its own washroom.

Taking a scalding bath, she scrubbed all traces of the Alpha from her body, and dressed in one of the simple blue tunics with gold stitching that she found in the wardrobe. She then ventured outside.

The pavilion was situated in some kind of village. It didn't look like any of the villages she'd seen in the kingdom, but that's what it had to be. Firm, hut-like structures, similar to Maddoc's pavilion scattered around the immediate area, and people milled around, walking between them and talking among themselves. The flat ground wasn't road or farmland, but solid dirt that had been smoothed over and set with something to prevent it from sticking to her slippers.

Nearby, tall, thick trees ran along the back of the structures, their branches intertwined so thickly that nothing could pass through them.

So it was true—Maddoc did have a base in Oakenshire Forest. Her breath caught as she noticed the dense tree barrier extending far into the distance. The base had to be huge.

She wandered around the immediate area, watching everyone carefully and examining the structures. Some of them were almost as large as Maddoc's, some of them were simple tents, others were shaped differently, but all of them were made securely and with lasting durability.

Strolling in whatever direction that interested her, she suddenly found herself in a busy open space with lots of people, all talking and calling out to each other. It had the bustling energy of a village square, and huts with wide windows offered different goods to trade. She stopped to watch the exchanges, noting that no money exchanged hands—one item was given for another, and in some cases items were just given freely.

Ana's curiosity grew. What a strange type of base. It didn't seem like the training ground for a band of hostile criminals who spent years terrorizing the kingdom. Why were these people here? Had Maddoc kidnapped them from their homes? They were clearly Allandis people, all different types and from different districts, but they didn't seem unhappy. They wore very simple clothes; a variety of tunics, pants, dresses, but it was difficult to tell their status'—farmer, tradesman, merchant, peasant—because they all wore similar clothing, materials, and colors.

As she kept walking, she was shocked to find children playing in one of the clearings. They ran round her to a nearby structure, circling round and zipping past her again trying to catch each other. Two of them jumped on one larger boy, all of them falling to the ground, rolling and laughing. She stared at them in amazement. What the hell were children doing here?

"I'm sorry, Princess Ana, are they disturbing you?"

A woman in a grey dress stood a few feet away, having just exited the nearby hut. A nervous expression dominated her pleasant features, and she leaned forward wringing her hands.

"No... No, of course not," Ana said, glancing at the children. "I was just surprised to see children here."

The woman relaxed and smiled. She turned her gaze to them. "I wouldn't have the strength to leave them, Your Majesty. I think I would die before giving up my children."

Ana frowned. "What do you mean? Why would you leave them at all?"

The woman shrugged. "For some, shame from peers is to be avoided at all costs, but for others, it's shame of self." She gave Ana a lopsided smile and turned to enter the hut, leaving Ana confused.

"Wait," Ana raised a hand. "You called me princess, how do you know I'm the princess."

She smiled. "It is obvious who you are." She gestured to Ana's hair. "You are unique in many ways, Your Majesty. We expected to see you here eventually."

Ana stared at her. "You did?"

The woman shot her a puzzled look. "Of course." She turned and made her way into the hut before Ana could think of anything else to say. The children's yelling caught Ana's attention, and she watched them as they dashed off again.

Ana continued her journey through the village and was surprised how many people smiled or nodded at her, some outright greeted her warmly. It didn't feel like when she usually visited a village—the people here didn't want to talk to her beyond an initial friendly greeting. It was refreshing.

She came across an opening in the edge of the village, where the dense wall of trees were exposed, and she took some time examining the trees and their network of branches. Her first impression had been right—there was no way anyone could physically go through it, at least not without causing themselves severe injury. Yet, there had to be a point where she and Maddoc entered. She couldn't recall anything about it now—she'd been too distressed to notice. But it was something to think about. If she could find the entrance, then she could escape or find ways to come back with the full force of the crown.

As midday approached, she noticed people gathering by the campfires that were dotted randomly around the base, stoking the fires and roasting or warming food. She passed one of the clearings as a large group were sitting down around the fire. "Princess Ana!" one of the men called. "Would you like to join us?"

Ana paused and raised her palms, shaking her head. "I don't mean to disturb you. Please, enjoy your meal."

"It's truly no problem, Princess," the young man said. "There is a rule 'ere that we all abide by, which is to offer a meal to anyone who chances to be passing by, even if they are heading toward their own camp."

The rest of the people around the fireplace nodded and beckoned her, and their smiles were so warm, she couldn't find any reason not to stay. It wasn't as though she knew her way back, or that she had access to food.

Ana headed to a space on the bench between the young man who had invited her and a young woman. Both looked to be about her age.

They both beamed as she sat down, then grinned at the other people at the camp who also seemed excited by her presence. The chatter began again, this time all of them talking to each other as they passed bowls and plates around the fireplace.

"We're having a simple stew, Princess," a large Alpha with twinkly blue eyes called from the right of the fire from where she sat, his deep voice soaring over the small din. "But it was made by my Marjorie, and I can guarantee you is one of the best stews you will ever have."

He grinned at the slim brown-skinned woman sitting a few seats along from him, embarrassment and pride shone on her face. "I'm sure it won't compare to the kind of meals you have at the palace," she said hastily. "We make the best of what we have here."

"I'm sure it will be lovely," Ana said warmly.

When the bowls of stew were passed out along with rolls of fresh, crusty bread, everyone bowed their head while the twinkly-eyed Alpha recited a short prayer of gratitude. Ana peeked at them all while their heads were lowered. She would be surprised if any of them were warriors. Women and young children sat among them, and even the men didn't look like any had been training to fight. Maybe Maddoc hadn't brought her to his base, after all. Maybe this was a village on the outskirts of the Oakenshire? The accent of the man beside her was familiar to a district she knew, but it wasn't strong. She had to find an appropriate time to ask questions, but didn't want to offend them when they were being so hospitable. She shook her head at herself—perhaps it's not so easy to just become a new Ana after all.

As she pondered, she spooned the stew into her mouth and was shocked. An intense explosion of flavor, heat, and aroma burst into her mouth and nose at the same time. "This is amazing," she said to the woman. "I've never tasted anything like this before. Are you a chef?"

She beamed. "No, we're exceptionally lucky to be able to grow such produce to flavor simple vegetables and meats."

"No," the Alpha said bluntly. "It is because she is a genius with a stove. I told her she should be a chef."

"I might have, if I could've gotten out from under you for five minutes," she muttered back.

Cries of "Oh, Mama!" came from at least three of the children, and Ana had to laugh with the rest of them.

She had to smile at the way the Alpha looked at his woman, and the way she grinned back at him. They were clearly in love. Her thoughts drifted back to her parents, and her mood descended. Lowering her face, she continued eating, keeping her attention on the food.

"How do you like the base so far?" the man next to her asked.

Ana's head shot up in surprise. So she *was* at a base. "I'm not sure," she said slowly. "It's different than what I expected. You all seem so...." She looked again at the people around the campfire, and suddenly began to see some similarities in their faces. "Are you all... family?"

The man nodded. "Yes, some of us are. All of the campfires are shared with other families."

Ana frowned. "What do you mean?"

"This base is organized into... Sort of, campfire circles. Each circle is surrounded by huts. So the families that live near that particular circle will share the campfire, and therefore share meals and the local well and anything that we need to live on."

"That makes sense," she said slowly. "I just didn't realize families would be here."

He nodded. "It's the only way we could have ever been together."

Ana frowned. "What do you mean?"

Before he could answer, one of the children on the other side of him demanded his attention.

Ana focused back on the fragrant stew, savoring each mouthful as she watched the families around the campfire. She began a mental guessing game of who was related to who, but soon she was distracted by their general demeanor. Everyone was grinning and smiling, teasing each other, yelling across the campfire and being told not to, chattering about their morning and their plans for the afternoon. They were... happy. And considering where they were, it was strange to her.

She turned to the young woman on the other side of her. "Do you know where we are?" she asked quietly.

The woman leaned in, her eyebrows rising. "Yes, the Oakenshire."

"And you came here… willingly?" she asked tentatively.

She nodded. "Of course, it wasn't as though we had anywhere else to go."

Ana frowned. "You couldn't live out in the kingdom? In one of the cities or villages?"

The woman shook her head, but her attention was drawn away by someone else as well.

Ana sat in her seat, with an empty bowl, wondering what was happening here. It felt drastically different to what she had read or what she had always heard the court say about Maddoc and his base and his people. These people were not warriors and they obviously weren't being held captive.

"You clearly enjoyed your stew, Princess." The young man returned his attention back to her and took her bowl. "Would you like some cake and wine?"

She nodded and as he poured, she asked, "What's your name?"

"Joe, Your Majesty."

"And your family name?"

The man's gaze remained on her cup, but his hand trembled slightly. "We are nameless here, Your Majesty. We don't have family names."

"Only according to the kingdom," the large man across the campfire corrected. "We very much have family names here."

Joe handed Ana her cup of wine and a round, fist-sized sponge cake, looking a little sheepish. "Yes, but I didn't want the princess to feel uncomfortable that we, the nameless, were using family names here."

The big man nodded. "Are you uncomfortable by that, Princess?"

At that, the entire campfire quietened. Not everyone turned to look at her, mostly the children did, but they were clearly all waiting for her answer.

The nameless were commoners who'd been stripped of their family names and all property and land by the crown for some reason. Usually it was because they failed to pay a debt or a failure to keep up with one's farmland or crops, or any number of other discrepancies that would cause a man to lose his livelihood. The nameless weren't quite criminals, since they didn't commit any major crimes, but they were also not seen as part of society. As such, while they weren't scorned the way criminals were, they didn't have the same rights, and were shunned and rejected most of the time.

Once a man became nameless, he could never regain his name unless it was re-awarded by the crown or a house representative, who had been awarded that power. Ana wasn't sure how frequently that happened, but she did know that once a man became nameless, it was common for his wife and children to seek another landowner who could provide for them. Being nameless as a family was never wise, and even a woman who loved her husband dearly would find it difficult to stay with him once he found himself in that situation, for the sake of the children. The fact these families were still together, united in their status as nameless, was quite extraordinary.

Ana lifted her shoulders. "I'm new here," she admitted. "I'm not sure exactly how this place works yet. But I am not here to upset the life you have. It makes no difference to me what you call yourselves."

"The nameless don't have any rights," one the children piped up. She had to be about five. "They're not 'llowed to have family names and have no value," she recited.

Her words tugged Ana's heart. She had taken on the burden of being nameless so young. "Maybe not in the kingdom," Ana said to her. "But you can tell me what you call yourselves."

"Well," Joe said, shifting uncomfortably in his seat. "Maddoc gave us permission to use our names or to choose new ones. Most of the families here have chosen new names, particularly when they have young children who may one day go into the kingdom, so they don't give names that have been listed as stripped."

Ana nodded in understanding. "That makes sense," she said softly. "I have no interest in reporting anyone. I'm sorry if my presence causes you discomfort."

Everyone around the campfire seem to relax slightly, all except the five-year-old. "We know you're not mean, Princess," she said, as if it was the most ridiculous thing. "Doc *said* you're nice."

"Doc?"

"Yes," she nodded solemnly. "He said you could never be mean. He said you're our—"

“All right, Trea,” the woman next to her said firmly. “That’s enough. I can see there is cake going to waste, that must mean you’re ill.”

Trea’s eyes opened so wide, and she stuffed her cake into her mouth without any further hesitation. Ana couldn’t help but laugh.

“I’m sorry, Your Majesty,” the woman said, turning to her. “Trea is one of our most outspoken, but she is right. We know you wouldn’t report us willingly, but you are bound by duties, just like we are.”

Ana smiled but before she could say anything the Alpha spoke again. She suspected he was the head of one of the families, possibly this particular camp.

"Indeed. You could never cause us discomfort by your presence. It's just the type of reaction people give us sometimes… It is hard for many of us not to be sensitive to what people say. And as Alice said, we don’t want to cause conflict with your duties or beliefs."

Ana glanced at all of them. “I understand. I do have some questions about this place.” The Alpha nodded at her, and gestured for her to speak, but suddenly she was nervous with them all staring at her.

She sipped her wine, and again was shocked at the fruity delicate flavor. She stared into her cup and then raised her head in astonishment. "What do you do to your food here?"

The entire camp laughed. "We do eat better here than when we were part of the kingdom," one of the men admitted.

Ana shook her head, laughing with them.

The rest of the hour was spent laughing and talking with them, answering questions about the palace and what it was like to be a princess. Trea in particular was fascinated by the knights. Ana, in turn, asked her own questions.

She discovered that the base was called Moonvale, and each family had arrived at different times, and therefore had varying knowledge of the place. Each family said Maddoc had brought them here when they were struggling in the kingdom, but all of them seemed reluctant to talk about their struggles, particularly in front of the children. They didn't know how many people were at the base, but guessed that there were more than thirty camps that catered to groups of families; attached to this one there were four.

Around the base, sections were cordoned off for growing produce, making and producing weapons, training, and schooling areas for the children. A fresh water stream ran through one part, and there was a river about an hour away if they needed it. Moonvale was full of tradesmen, and the twinkly-eyed Alpha, called Conrad, explained that their knowledge of trade was the base's biggest strength. They had bakers, builders, carpenters, plumbers, farmers, tailors… all the skills needed to build a successful community, and that it was the philosophy to share and trade freely.

Ana's mind reeled at all the information. Their answers caused even more questions, but she couldn't figure out a way to ask them. They were very complimentary of Maddoc, but they had to know all the things he'd done. How could they condone it?

As discussion moved on to other topics, she examined them again, and they were completely at ease. No worry adorned their faces. But she forced herself to be objective. This may not be representative of the entire base.

Soon everyone was ready to continue with their afternoon activities, and Ana rose to bid them farewell.

"I don't mean to be forward, Your Majesty," Joe said, rising with her. "But it would be nice to have you back to visit us. I know you'll be busy, but you're welcome for a meal with us anytime, and we'd very much like to see you again." The rest of the families nodded, and little Trea and her brother both yelled in agreement. Ana laughed, grinning at all of them. "Of course, I would love to return."

As everyone got up, Joe pulled her aside to give her directions back to Maddoc's pavilion and pressed a flask of wine in her hands. "We are camp sixteen," he said. "If you ask anyone where we are, you'll be able to get back 'ere."

"Thank you. I'm very grateful for your company today."

"You're the one who is a princess," Joe remarked. "Trea is bursting to tell everyone when she has her classes in three days. I'm not sure we'll be able to calm her down."

She laughed with him. "Who did she mean when she said Doc?"

Joe's smiled widened. "Maddoc."

Ana's mouth dropped open. "She speaks to him? He… speaks to her?"

Joe nodded, chuckling. "She won't leave him alone when he visits. She insists she wants to be a highcloak, so she follows him around to 'protect him.'"

"A highcloak?"

"Yes, they are…" Joe thought for a moment. "They are the most visible and recognizable members of Maddoc's guild. They tend to be the ones in direct conflict in the kingdom. They wear cloaks."

Ana shook her head in confusion. "Guild?"

Joe nodded. "The ones who support Maddoc. There are active members who do things out in the kingdom, then the passive members like us."

Help Maddoc? "I'm not sure I—" Suddenly she remembered the wedding. All of Maddoc's warriors wore black cloaks. She quickly sobered. "You mean the highcloaks are Maddoc's army. They kill people."

Joe's smile faded and he sighed. "Yes, I suppose you could see it that way, but there is more than one side to a story, Your Majesty."

"So I keep being told," Ana muttered. She shook her head in disbelief. So not only were these people aware of Maddoc's behavior and attacks on Allandis, they condoned it and were encouraging their children to aspire to it. The heavy disappointment dampened Ana's mood.

Joe touched her arm, seeming to sense the change. "Please come back and spend time with us," he said quietly. "The more you visit, the more you'll learn."

Ana gave him a warm smile and said she would, but she knew she'd already learned all she needed to know about this place.

After thanking the camp again for their hospitality, Ana strolled through the village, seeing it in a new light. There were plenty of smiles here, relaxed people who had been cast out of Allandis society, or those who chose to leave, conducting their business as part of a community, and she had to appreciate that. The tight tension of hate toward Maddoc that had kept her hard inside, unraveled slowly the more she watched the happiness around her, but a deep sadness for these people replaced it. Maddoc was manipulating them. He was using them to grow his future warriors and murderers out of the sight and reach of Allandis Law. It was despicable. And every time she thought of little wide-eyed Trea, so eager to became a warrior, so eager to kill, she knew it was wrong.

As the sky grew dusky, a man approached her dressed in layers of clothes similar to Maddoc's. "Your Majesty," he greeted. "Please follow me to return to your hut."

Ana frowned. "How did you find me? Did Maddoc send you to get me?"

He shook his head. "He will be arriving back to base soon, and he would prefer it if you were in his pavilion when he does."

Ana's eyes widened. "Does he know I'm out here, in the camp?"

"He knew you would probably explore."

"And you were sent to find me?"

"No, I have been watching all day. But now is the time to return back to the pavilion."

So Maddoc ordered him to watch her all day. Unbelievable. "How did I not see you?"

At that, the guard did not respond and Ana pursed her lips in understanding. She hadn't seen him because he hadn't wanted to be seen. He had most likely been following the moment she left the tent.

"Please, Your Majesty," he urged. "The skies are darkening rapidly and we need to return. I very much doubt you know the way."

Ana lifted a hand gesturing for him to lead the way, and she followed him back to Maddoc's pavilion.

When she was back inside, exhaustion hit her hard. How far had she walked today? The base was bigger than it looked no matter how far she walked. Out of curiosity, she peeked outside the pavilion to see if the huts here were arranged the same way as the family camps. But there weren't as many structures for her to discern. She exited the pavilion and walked around the whole structure, but the nearest clearing with a campfire was a little way away, with very few people nearby.

"Good evening, Princess."

She turned to see a man standing a few feet away in the semidarkness, and she stiffened. He wore a cloak.

"Welcome to our guild."

Ana did not return his smile. "I am not willingly visiting."

"I'm sure that you will be happy to stay once you give us a chance," the man said.

Ana peered at him. His voice seemed friendly enough and he wasn't carrying any weapons. "Is that what you did? Give this place a chance."

"Sort of. I haven't been here long," he admitted. "I'm still learning how everything works."

"You're part of the guild?" Ana asked tentatively.

The man nodded.

"So you are a new… highcloak?"

The man hesitated, then gestured to the campfire. They began to stroll toward it. "I am new, yes. I'm still in training."

"Why did you join?"

The man shrugged. "I thought it might be a good way to get back at the royals." A grit entered his tone. "I know the guild works against the royal assembly, I wanted to be part of that."

A strange unease worked in Ana. This was the first person she'd met, apart from Maddoc, who had real hostility toward the assembly. Although she assumed that was the point of the guild, and the reason why Maddoc created this base, she suddenly realized that she hadn't experienced any hatred or hostility from anyone in the camp, whether it was toward the assembly, her, or each other. Maybe it was just the highcloaks that held the hostility.

They reached the campfire and settled down on a bench nearby.

"Why do you want to get back at them?" she asked, unsure if she wanted to hear the answer.

When the man looked to her, his eyes held a hardness that didn't reflect the easy-going nature of his tone. "They are evil, greedy tyrants. I know you probably don't see it," he said, shooting her a dark look, "but the rest of us have to suffer because of them. I want to be able to fight back and make an actual difference."

"But what if someone gets hurt?"

"I hope they do! They have hurt me and my family; it is only right they get what they are due."

Ana kept her eyes on the campfire as it flickered, unsure if she wanted to ask how his family was hurt. She wasn't sure if she was prepared to hear the supposed cruelty of the royal assembly without any evidence that it was true. There was plenty of evidence of Maddoc's men and what they did; she'd seen the files and studied them. She wasn't sure it was worth arguing with a man who was intent on harm, especially when she was a princess.

When she didn't respond, the man sighed. "I suppose this is not a great introduction to the base," he said sheepishly. "Sometimes my manners can get misplaced. I'm sorry if I seem rude to you, Your Majesty. It is very hard to be unemotional about some of this. I will say the base are excited you are here. You have been the talk of every camp."

The hardness had melted from the man's eyes, and Ana chose to give him a small smile.

"Another day gone," he said on a sigh. "Another day to question our existence here in the middle of this forest. Has it been strange for you?"

Ana shrugged. "A little. But it's felt more like a village. Everyone is very friendly."

The man nodded. "Almost everyone," he said pointedly gesturing to Maddoc's pavilion.

Ana laughed, nodding.

A familiar whipping sound flashed across the air, and the man jolted, yelling out. Gasps and muffled murmurs filled the air, and everyone stilled.

Ana leaned toward the man but suddenly saw an arrow stuck out of his thigh, blood creeping along his pants from the wound, eating up the circumference around the arrow.

A violent blend of horror and fear crashed into Ana immediately and she screamed, her body frozen. Heart pounding, Ana's mind swarmed with memories of the wedding. Squeezing her hands into fists and digging her nails into her hand hard, she forced herself to remember she was not there. The man blinked rapidly, his head straight ahead and his eyes filled with fear. Taking a breath, she followed the man's line of sight.

Maddoc stormed toward them, a bow in his hand, his face solemn and his eyes dark.

Ana could make no sounds. What was she supposed to do? Maddoc looked furious once again, and this time she didn't know why. But before she could do or decide anything, Maddoc reached them.

He grabbed the highcloak and dragged him up off the bench. "Were you not given specific instructions regarding the princess?" he bellowed.

The fear on the man's face made Ana want to look away, but she couldn't.

"Yes," he rasped. "But she looked lost so I—"

"If you cannot follow instructions, you will die," Maddoc shouted over him. "It doesn't matter whether it's by my arrow or a royal assembly blade. I would almost prefer it to be my arrow because then you're not putting other men in danger." He threw the man down, and he bounced off the bench and onto the floor, the arrow still protruding. "You will be transferred."

He turned to Ana and swooped her up in his arms before walking away.

Ana clung to the Alpha, her mouth dry at the exchange. Thankfully, the fear that overwhelmed her dulled when she was against him, and she quickly calmed, sinking into the security of his arms. She didn't want to find comfort in him—he was the damn reason she was fearful in the first place—but when he was holding her, when he touched her, he contented her in some way, and she had no choice but to lean into that now.

"Maddoc."

She lifted her head to see another Alpha approaching. This one was as large as Maddoc, scruffy grey beard and curly grey hair.

"I gave specific instructions, Griff," Maddoc thundered.

"I know." The other Alpha held up his arm. "I know, I just want to make sure you are all right." He struggled to find his next words. In the end he just shrugged. "You have never shot any of the highcloaks outside of training."

"I have never had my Omega here at the base before and had anyone directly disobey orders," Maddoc shot back. "This is what will happen to anyone that does. It is your job to make sure they do as they're told, Griff." He shot the Alpha a dark look, a warning in his tone. "Do your fucking job."

As they entered his pavilion, she struggled to be released from his hold, but he carried her straight to the bedroom.

"So you are refusing to talk to me, but you will talk to him!" Maddoc thundered, throwing her down on the bed. "And *laugh* with him!"

Ana gripped on to the bed and glared at him. So it wasn't about her safety.

"This silence of yours is unacceptable, Analisa! If you will not speak to me, you will not speak to anyone!"

Ana decided to ignore him. She fixed herself on the bed, tucking her legs underneath her body.

"You think I do not know that you left the pavilion today after I told you not to? That you talked to some of my people and explored the base?" Maddoc's eyes burned. "I allowed you to do that so you can be comfortable here. And what do I get in return? You laughing and talking with someone else while I get silence!"

Ana's mouth tightened. She shifted onto her bottom and then opened her legs, bearing her pussy to him, defiance in her eyes. That was what he'd had in return—her body, multiple times last night.

Maddoc growled, deep, gritty and agitated, clearly understanding the meaning, but unable to stop himself from being aroused, for his scent changed as it flooded the room. "That is *mine*, I get that anyway."

Except… he didn't. Not since he made that rule this morning that he wouldn't fuck her. Ana couldn't help the smile that spread across her face, but it only incensed Maddoc, who seemed to be able to read her easily.

He grabbed her legs and pulled her down the bed toward him, and then roughly pulled off her tunic and grabbed a rope from a small table nearby. He used it to bind her wrists together and attached them to the head of the bed. Ana winced at the pain that still lingered on her back, but Maddoc didn't notice. His anger, present in his scent, worked through her body, affecting her the same way that it did in the woodlands. By the time he climbed off the bed, her nipples were pebbling, and the tingling between her legs made her hum.

Maddoc yanked off his clothes and stood at the end of the bed watching her, his cock already bulging.

Ana watched it sway, the urge strong to press her nose against it, to lick and suck its length. She kept her legs apart, ready for when the Alpha decided to descend and thrust into her. But he didn't.

Maddoc grabbed his shaft and worked his fist up and down, his eyes running over her naked form. A jarring annoyance barreled into Ana and she frowned, lifting her head to see what he was doing. The more he twisted his fist around his cock, the more aroused she became, but he didn't approach her. Within moments, her need was unbearable. The Alpha's musky scent filled the room, but none of it saturated her, his growls and lidded look of pleasure were not caused by her body, and she couldn't even reach him to force him to take action. All she could do was lie there, her slick streaming onto the bed as the Alpha found his release in his hand. Even when he came, he did not mark her, and the sight of his seed dripping from between his fingers, utterly wasted, had her wailing in annoyance.

Maddoc went to the washroom and started filling the bath. Ana lay there as her arousal lingered, infuriated by his offensive actions. But as her mind cleared, she was confused by her anger. There was no doubt she wanted him to touch her. And not just touch her, but hold her down and fuck her as savagely and passionately as he always had, bringing her the twin peak of pleasure and pain until only bliss remained.

But she'd always thought that if she had the choice, she wouldn't want it, even if it was presented to her as an option.

Clearly her attraction to him ran deeper than that, and for the first time she thought back to her time with Ryden. It had been easy to say no to him, to avoid his touch, to push him away. What made Maddoc different? The question made her uneasy, but she couldn't ignore it anymore.

Even when Maddoc had just carried her to the tent, there was nothing he did that was sexual, and yet she took comfort from being in his arms. Why? As she pondered, Maddoc returned from the washroom.

She watched him get dressed, unable to help admiring his enormous, muscled form. His black hair was slightly wet from the bath and his beard was a little overgrown, but that made him even sexier. The tingle between her legs strengthened again just watching him, and she pulled her eyes away confused. Something had to be causing this attraction between them and she had to figure it out so she could stop it. She could not be attracted to her father's murderer, to the man who terrorized the kingdom.

Maddoc approached the bed and leaned over to untie her wrists but was careful not to touch her. He loomed over her, his eyes softening as he examined her face. "I will punish you as necessary… but I am still very glad you are here, Analisa."

She blinked up at him, a warmth blooming in her chest, but she dragged her eyes away from him.

"Good night." Maddoc leaned up off the bed and headed to the exit of the pavilion.

Ana pushed herself up to her elbows and watched him leave in disbelief. He wasn't even going to spend the night in here? She cursed and dropped down onto the bed. Good. At least she would be able to sleep in peace.

But as hard as she tried, the torture of the intense arousal he caused took a long time to subside. She yearned for his heat and his scent and the security of his hold, and she was infuriated that he withheld them.

SEVEN

ANA

The next morning, Ana woke to the Alpha lifting her out of bed. She immediately tried to snuggle into his chest, keen for the comfort she had missed all night, but Maddoc bathed her, applied the salve to her back, and dressed her without saying a word.

Strangely, he dressed her in a long olive dress that was typical commoner wear. The coarse material scratched her skin but she found she liked the style and fit. He pushed hard sandals on her feet and brushed her hair so that it fell loosely over her shoulders.

Picking her up again, he carried her out of the pavilion toward the clearing she was in yesterday. A number of highcloaks waited for them by the campfire, and as soon as Maddoc joined them, they all started heading in a specific direction.

Ana took the opportunity to enjoy being in Maddoc's arms. She hated that she did, but it wasn't as though she had a choice. When she pressed her cheek against his chest and sighed, he looked down on her, his beard twitching. She scowled and turned her face in toward his chest so he couldn't see her face.

When she turned her face back out again, they had left the camp and were trudging through bushes and bramble and leaves. Ana cursed inwardly. She had missed how they exited the base, and didn't even know which direction they had headed in to access it.

She remained alert, trying to make note of what she saw, but all around them was greenery and bushes. It was impossible to pinpoint anything in particular.

Finally, they came to a more spacious area where horses awaited them. Maddoc climbed the same huge, black horse he had ridden to the base and placed Ana on the saddle in front of him, a thick arm around her securing her against his body.

They rode for a long time, possibly even longer than when they had arrived here, but Ana had been so disorientated she couldn't tell. Being on the horse for so long, she began to ache, and right when as she thought she couldn’t take any more, the horses angled to the left and the forest began to thin out. They rode into a medium-sized town and stopped outside of a tavern.

Maddoc dismounted and lifted Ana off the horse, but this time allowed her to stand, even though his arm remained around her.

They all headed to the outskirts of the town, toward the fields and took position in a small cluster of abandoned buildings near one of the fields.

The highcloaks clearly had a routine. Some of them positioned themselves farther down, crouched behind a broken wall. The ones with Maddoc rolled a blanket underneath the windows to kneel on, propped up a bow next to the window, lay their swords on the floor in front of their knees, and took out magnifying lenses to look through.

Maddoc rolled a blanket on the floor and knelt down, pulling Ana to stand next to him, his arm around her hips. She didn't need to kneel.

"I have been watching these fields for a while," he began in a low voice. "There are eight farmers across the entirety of the land, but in this quarter, only two manage it. Their families help them maintain their crops." He gave her a magnifying lens, and she took it, confused about why he was telling her this. Through the lens she saw men, women, and children working on the land.

"These farmers don't own this land," Maddoc said, taking back the lens. "They used to, but they were forced to sell when the owner of the neighboring lands threatened their family if they didn't."

Ana made a face. That shouldn't have happened. Anyone forcing someone to sell through threats should be dealt with by the crown. The farmers could have petitioned for a hearing with the king.

"Since they have been bought, they have not been able to meet the quota of crops demanded by the new landowners," Maddoc continued. "They have struggled mainly for two reasons; the land is too big for the two farmers and their families to successfully manage, and the crops that the landowners want do not grow well on this kind of land."

Ana nodded. These landowners seemed like they were being unnecessarily unreasonable.

"At the beginning of this quarter, the landowners told the farmers that if they did not meet their requirements, they would be made nameless."

Ana shot Maddoc a sharp look. That was not the way things were supposed to go. She had read the boring rules around landownership, farming, and crops when she had been researching him. It was completely unlawful to threaten namelessness for those reasons. Besides, only the crown could make someone nameless, not some noble with an ego.

Maddoc met her gaze, but she was unable to read the look in his eyes. He gestured back toward the fields. "Watch."

Ana turned to see horses approaching the field where the families were frantically working. There were at least fifteen horses!

A dark tremble drifted at the pit of her stomach. Something was wrong. It was impossible for fifteen people to own one piece of land, so what were so many doing here?

The horses stopped by the field, and the riders called out to the farmers and their families. They reluctantly all stood together while they conversed.

Ana watched closely, wishing she could hear what was being said between them. She hoped the farmers were threatening them with the crown and Allandis Law that had been so painstakingly put together to avoid abuses of this kind.

Suddenly, one of the people on the horses drew a sword and pointed it at the farmers. Ana tensed, unable to believe the sight in front of her. Surely, this person would not attack anyone in broad daylight simply for not providing crops on time.

The families in the field shuffled on their feet, and then one of them began running across the field as fast as they possibly could. Ana watched in shock, hoping that he would be able to find some help before the rest of them were hurt, but suddenly, he fell to the ground, sprawled out. She gasped and clung to the edge of the window.

Looking back at the men on horses, she saw that one of them held a bow and arrow.

The remainder of the families, huddled closer together, but the rider moved the bow and arrow and aimed it at them.

Some of the riders dismounted and headed toward the families,

"This is the way they make them nameless," Maddoc murmured, as the riders approached the farmers' families. "After this, they will have no status in society and no one will believe them." It wasn't clear what they were doing, but it was clear that it was violent. Some of the farmers fell to the ground, some of them were pushed until they became a big jumble of people and she couldn't determine what was happening.

Ana shook her head in horror, but just as she was about to say something, Maddoc handed her the magnifying lens again and gestured that she looked through it.

Nerves rolled in her stomach, but she lifted the lens to her eyes. The sight sickened her.

The riders were much better dressed than the farmers; it was easy to tell who was who, and they were carrying out the most horrific acts.

One man was driving his sword into the twitching torso of a man lying on the ground, another had a woman on her knees and held her head as he pushed his cock into her face, a third man had a young girl on her knees, gripping her ass as he pounded into her, her panties tangled at her knees, and yet another man was doing the same to a young boy. Another older boy was topless and being whipped on his bare skin as he knelt. An older man, possibly one of the farmers, was watching in horror while another one of the riders stood by talking to him.

"You can increase the distance by turning the dial here," Maddoc said, pushing her finger onto a dial on the magnifying lens.

Ana wrenched the magnifying lens away from her face, glaring at him. Why did he bring her to witness this? If he knew it was going to happen, he could have called the crown and asked for support for the farmers from the king, even in the current state of the kingdom, somebody in the court would be able to help.

Maddoc watched her closely. "It is to help you see who they are," he said. "You will recognize them."

Ana's stomach dropped, the sickening feeling creeping into her throat. Hesitantly, she raised the magnifying glass again, and turned the dial.

She gasped at the sight of the faces in front of her. She recognized all of the riders. They were from House Thorneshaw. It was Everard who she'd met at Ryden's house who was talking to the farmer, but the man he was speaking to had been beaten at some point. His mouth was full of blood, his face bruised, and all he could do was watch what was happening with despair. The men who were raping those women and children were married men—they were well respected in court. Thick dark blood ran down the back of the thighs of the young girl on her knees. The younger boy who was being whipped, was screaming. Even though she couldn't hear him, she could tell he was yelling at the top of his lungs. And it was a woman who was whipping him. A woman who had congratulated Ana on her tour only a few days ago. It looked as though she might be laughing.

Ana swung the lens over to the horses, to the men who had not dismounted, and the nausea hit her harder when she realized they were knights—trained knights who belonged to the house and they held weapons, including bows and arrows, presumably to stop the commoners from fighting back.

Ana lowered the magnifying lens. She was going to be sick.

"This land belongs to House Thorneshaw," Maddoc said. "They acquired it legally."

Ana took a halting breath and shook her head, unable to speak, even if she wanted to. It cannot be legal to obtain land in that way; Allandis Law prevented it.

"They obtained it after petitioning the king in court six months ago." Maddoc paused. "During that hearing, he gave the house the right to declare the farmers nameless if they did not uphold the crop schedule. You may have been in attendance."

Ana squeezed her eyes shut, unable to deal with the horror of it. Her father had allowed this to happen? She had to remember if she'd been in court that day, to try to remember his reasoning for it, but she couldn't think right now, people were being abused and destroyed in front of her eyes, and it was agitating her to the point of tears.

"Analisa," Maddoc said. "We came here to intervene. Normally we would have intervened already, but I wanted you to see what would happen. It is the same every time, no matter how many times we try to stop them, or give them chances to stop, all they do is bring more knights to fight us, and sometimes they kill the commoners. So we usually intervene before it gets to this stage. We cannot do nothing." Ana looked at him, searching his eyes. They were fierce, black and soulless. He was going to kill them.

She had been raised to believe that everyone should have a fair chance to defend themselves using Allandis Law. But the court was the one who gave these men the license to behave like this, so they were not acting unlawfully in the eyes of the court, they were not acting illegally. The crime of rape and whipping were still illegal, but it was difficult even for nobles to be punished for those crimes, let alone members of a royal house.

So she said nothing, and Maddoc nodded at his men.

She jumped at the whipping noises from the arrows shooting from the bows of the highcloaks next to her, and the ones who had been crouching on the outer parts of the structure, charged onto the field.

Maddoc turned Ana from the window and pushed her toward a highcloak waiting behind them. “Raine will take you back to Moonvale. I will be back soon.”

Ana was too numb to respond, her mind still trying to grapple with what she had seen. The woman he pushed her toward smiled uneasily as she took Ana's hand and led her out of the structure and back to the horses.

Although Raine was on the small side, she was strong enough to push Ana up onto her horse.

She climbed up behind her and rode back the way they came. Ana's mind whirled trying to make sense of any reason why a royal house would behave that way and do those things to commoners. Why would they rape when they have wives? Why would they inflict so much pain on children? Why would they even seek permission to make commoners nameless on ridiculous demands?

She took a sharp breath. If that was how they made people nameless… Was that what happened to Conrad? And Joe? And Trea’s family? The thought made her shudder and the nausea almost overwhelmed her.

She had never had any reason not to hold the houses in high regard, each of them had their strengths as a house, and each have had a strong and honorable history. All kings held the houses in high regard in terms of their integrity. Her father couldn't have known that this was going to happen.

Her skin crawled at the idea that she’d been in the same room as Everard only a few days ago, discussing giving him her children. She would have sentenced her child to a marriage with a house that had highly corrupt individuals, and it could never have been reversed. Yes, it had to be just these individuals, she finally decided. It wasn’t possible for everyone in House Thorneshaw to behave this way.

And yet, it was unsettling that Maddoc knew it was going to happen. He had been so sure that he arrived early enough to make her watch.

By the time they reached the dense part of the forest, the horror had settled deep in her bones.

The female highcloak took her hand and led her through the bushes and trees and shrubbery, navigating back to the base and Maddoc's pavilion. Ana let her mind go blank, unwilling to think about it anymore until she was able to make sense of it.

"Maddoc would prefer if you stayed in the pavilion today," the woman said, somewhat nervously. "He will be back just after sundown."

Ana nodded and trudged inside, once again alone with her troublesome thoughts.

Ana debated for the rest of the afternoon whether she should break her silence to speak to Maddoc about this issue. Although she had made her vow in honor of her father and Ryden, she also made a promise that she would not abandon the people—that she would still be Princess Ana, who would uphold everything that the crown stood for—even in this environment. She wanted to know how often this happened, if all the attacks were this bad, what happened to the land after the family was made nameless. Had any royal house member been caught doing what they were doing, had this been reported to the crown? All of these very relevant questions would help her understand how serious the problem was, but even if she asked Maddoc, could she trust what he said? Yes, he had shown her an atrocity that happened in front of her own eyes, but she didn't have any further information and she didn't want to be manipulated again. She said she would take all the steps she could to find information out for herself, and that was what she had to try to do. Besides, how did she know that this would have happened if her father were alive and in power? Maybe it only happened because he was dead.

So, she changed out of her clothing and paced the pavilion, the thoughts revolving in her mind as she resolved that she would try to find out more once she escaped this place, but she would not speak to Maddoc, at least for now.

At sundown, a meal was brought to her by the same guard who led her back to Maddoc's pavilion the day before, and just as she finished it, Maddoc entered.

He looked wild, that darkness in his eyes, splashes of blood over him, and gashes scoring his arms. He strode straight to her and pulled her into a hard kiss, his fingers digging into the back of her head, his mouth claiming hers in that eager and desperate way he always did, and instantly she was alive.

Kissing him back, Ana drifted into the sweet cloud of arousal that always surrounded them, needing to be comforted by him, and now knowing he needed to be comforted too. For the first time, Ana could almost understand his need for her when his eyes were so dark.

As their kiss softened, Maddoc sucked on her bottom lip and nipped at her top as he pulled away. "Are we fucking today?" he asked bluntly.

Ana almost scowled at the coarseness of his words. He could have simply asked if she was speaking to him, but then she realized there was amusement in his eyes, and his beard twitched as he took in her expression.

She smiled and he kissed her again before turning away, chuckling. He left the tent, and much to Ana's disappointment, did not return for the rest of the night.

❖

Unfortunately for Ana's theory, the same thing happened for the next three days.

Maddoc dressed her like a commoner, and then they traveled into the Kingdom of Allandis to different districts to watch the abuse of commoners by members of royal houses. The first day she watched members of Goldfrost gleefully set fire to a house of a family who could not pay the increased tax; the family was still inside.

Maddoc showed her the family's request to the court to lower the tax, but their petition came back denied, signed by the king three months ago.

The next day she watched House Villemore tie two very young children to the back of a horse because they had been picking and eating fruit growing in the garden of a house that no one lived in. They couldn't have been much older than Trea, and their parents were begging on their knees. Ana hadn't been able to bear it and screamed that Maddoc do something immediately. Thankfully, he already had men intervene before anything happened, but it shook her to her core that anyone could do that. That was the first time she cried herself to sleep, angry and upset that these were people she knew committing these crimes, people she had sat across from in the court, people whose homes she's visited, who she made small talk with, and who she'd studied and looked up to.

The third day, it was House Redcrest. A number of men and women arrived in a town to stone five men to death for getting into a brawl in the local tavern. Ana was shocked. Maddoc explained that the knights who reported to the crown had "sold" House Redcrest the opportunity to punish them. The Redcrest members turned up in their finest wear, as if it were some sort of entertainment event, and had brought their own hand-picked, jewel-encrusted stones to throw. Looking at their faces as they lined the commoner men up against the wall, it was clear the Redcrest nobles were excited about it. One of the men even had an erection. It was disgusting. Ana actually vomited on the way back to the camp this time.

There was no more reasoning or defending any of it, even the fact that her father had approved some of what was happening was extremely suspect, but she was still reluctant to believe it. Her father had been an upstanding man. How could he have approved this knowing what was happening, both him and her mother? It couldn't be possible that the kingdom was so grossly corrupt after everything her parents and Milly had taught her.

She clung to the fact that her father was now dead and she couldn't ask him, and that it was possible that all of this was a result of them having no king—the houses taking advantage of the lack of structure. This was what the monarchy was supposed to prevent, after all. She wondered if this was what her parents had been hiding from her, and if so, how they intended to keep it hidden? If the monarch was truly giving the royal houses opportunities to break the law and commit such crimes, she would have found out eventually. Both she and Ryden would have. Or, maybe Ryden had known? Maybe that was why he was insisting her father was unfit.

Each night, Maddoc came to the pavilion with his dark eyes and bloodied and scratched body, then kissed her like his life depended on it, and she started to look forward to that time each day. Even though the days were horrific, she wanted him near her, the strange comfort he brought, and she found herself agitated until he arrived. Part of her wished that he returned with her back to the base, but she was confused by her desire for him to be safe, as well as her deepening attraction to him. On the third night, after he left, she desperately wished that he hadn't been the one to kill her father. Or that he had been able to explain everything he was now showing her. She knew she wouldn't have believed him, but she wished things had gone differently, because with the way things stood, she couldn't let herself feel anything for him—his arrow in her father's neck denied her the chance to ever confront her father.

She woke in a gloomy mood on the fourth day, and as Maddoc dressed her, he must have sensed it. He grabbed her chin and tilted her eyes up to his, searching them. "These horrors are hard to see, Analisa. You have done well. I only have two more things to show you, today and tomorrow, and then you don't have to watch them again."

She nodded, but what use was that? Ana wanted to say. Not seeing them didn't mean they weren't happening.

He pressed his lips on hers, and she sighed with great relief and pleasure that she didn't have to wait until evening for his kiss. She kissed him back, eager for his tongue and the way it dominated her mouth, sending sparks of pleasure all around her body. Since he'd stopped touching her, the smallest things about him affected her greatly, and she took whatever she could.

She whimpered as he pulled away and pressed his mouth against her ear. "Talk to me, Analisa."

Swallowing, Ana battled with herself at the sudden request, but ended up saying nothing. Maddoc growled and lifted her into his arms.

Today they went to the central city.

Because of the quality of the gown that Maddoc dressed her in, Ana had already guessed they would be heading toward the nobles' residences.

For some reason, being among the nobles again, especially now after what she'd seen some of the royal house members do, made her nervous. Everything in the central city was much closer together. It was harder for Maddoc and his men to navigate and if they were caught, it would be very difficult to escape. By the same token, if Ana wanted, she could scream and tell everyone who she was and whom she was with, and there was the possibility she could escape. But she had seen too much now, and didn't know whom she could trust. She didn't even know what was happening between the royal houses and the crown. With her father dead, was she any safer among the royal houses than with Maddoc? He wasn't even touching her anymore, which was becoming bitterly annoying each day.

"The houses have now decided that I am too much of a threat to remain alive," Maddoc said, as they entered the upstairs room in a popular tavern visited by nobles and royals. "They have agreed among them that I must be killed and you must be recovered at all costs, and the house that is successful at doing so will marry you off and he will be the next king."

Ana nodded, her expression glum. That was the kind of plan that the houses would agree amongst themselves.

"They haven't made any real effort to kill me over the years," Maddoc said. He sat down on one of the couches and pulled her into his lap. "They needed someone to blame for their crimes, and I and my people were the perfect choice—since those who join me are already people they have eliminated from society. They have no problem accusing us all for being outlaws and criminals. I will admit, some of my men are criminals. In the beginning I took whomever I could. But now, I do not abide senseless killing or men and women who only want to commit crimes no matter the cost to others. I gladly will kill any royal and noble who abuses their power, but I have no interest in senseless killing."

Ana watched his eyes as he spoke, his voice determined and low, his expression grave. For the first time, she noticed a sadness embedded in his anger for the situation, and she wondered how long he had been doing this. It had to be heartbreaking to see this happening all the time. When she thought about Moonvale… There were potentially over one hundred families who lived there. On a much larger scale, however, Maddoc had not saved that many. And in the meantime while this was happening, she'd been tucked away in her library reading stories. How right he'd been that first night; she had been so woefully ignorant about everything. And even now the houses treated her like some kind of vessel and shell to bear the next heir… just as he said.

A rough finger under her chin brought her back to the moment; Maddoc's eyes were alive on her. "You cannot take on the horror of this, Analisa. I'm not showing you this for you to be sad. I'm showing you so you understand. This will not be our life."

She didn't know how to respond to that. He was planning some life with them together, and in the meantime she was just confused.

He leaned in, pressing his mouth against her ear. "I miss your pussy, Analisa."

The gravelly tone of his voice made her breath hitch.

"I think I will have you climax in my mouth tonight. A treat for good behavior." When he pulled away, his eyes were sparkling, and she had to smile. He was so handsome, and she instantly wondered what he was like before he knew about this darkness that plagued the kingdom.

His hand inched up her thigh, and she pressed her knees together, desperate not to become soaking wet while in this room.

Maddoc chuckled, and Ana averted her eyes, only to remember that they weren't alone. His highcloaks stood stationed at the windows and doors, and although most were ignoring them, Raine stared at them with great interest.

"They're not heading to the right room," one of the highcloaks said suddenly.

Maddoc sat up. "What do you mean?"

The man standing by the back door gestured to the window. "I just saw them entering through this door, which means they're not coming through here."

"Then where are they going?" Maddoc growled.

"They're coming to this floor," another highcloak said.

Griff cracked open the door to the room that they came through and peeked through for a long moment and then closed it. "They are next door," he said quietly. "We have to be extremely quiet; the walls are thin. Our contact must have put us here because she wasn't exactly sure where they'd go. Perhaps she knew they might change venue."

Ana's breath became unsteady as she realized she would be able to hear everything instead of seeing it, and suddenly she wasn't so sure she wanted to listen. Maddoc stood slowly and placed her down, then took her hand and led her to the adjoining wall to listen. All the highcloaks stood listening.

There was a shuffling and closing the door, heavy boots walking around the room.

"This is the fifth we've had," a deep voice said irritably. "It had better lead to some good results."

"Or what," another voice shot back. "Do you have anything better?"

Heat drained from Ana's face. That was Aldous from Redcrest. Suddenly, she was extremely uneasy about what she was going to hear. Aldious always seemed like a kind and generous man. She braced herself.

"You're only giving him this amount of leeway because you want something when he becomes king. I don't even know why he is our best chance."

"Who would you have instead?" Aldous asked. "You? Do you know anything about the court or about the people? You'd be run off the throne before you even sat down."

The door opened and a series of shuffling and dragging followed before something hit the wall that they were listening against. Ana almost squealed, a tiny squeak bursting from her throat as she jumped.

Maddoc locked eyes with her, both of them frozen, but it seemed those on the other side heard nothing. Maddoc carefully lifted Ana back into his arms and held her against chest. Immediately, her nerves calmed.

"Where is Maddoc?" a new voice said. It sounded as though there were multiple people in the room now, just by the amount of footsteps.

Whoever was against the wall, shifted. "I don't know," he wheezed. It sounded as though he had trouble breathing, and his voice was thick, as though his mouth was full of blood or his tongue was swollen. "I've told you so many times before," he groaned. "Why won't you believe me?"

"Because it's impossible for you not to know where he is when he has been sighted by your property so many times," the man growled. "So we're going to ask you over and over again until you tell us what the fuck we want to know!"

"I don't know, I swear to you! I don't know where he is, I don't know where he's been, and I don't know where he's going to be. The sightings must be because he frequently goes past my property. But I don't know him."

Ana glanced at Maddoc. His jaw was rock hard.

"Tell us where he is!"

A loud thud hit the wall, and the man cried out.

"We can do this all day," came Aldous' low tone. "And now we have the use of the king's guard, we can make it as painful and as crippling as we want."

Ana closed her eyes, willing away the nausea that rose. Why did they have access to the king's guard? The king's guard were only supposed to protect the king. But then, she didn't know the rules around what happened in this scenario when the king was assassinated and there was no heir.

"I swear," the man wheezed. "I swear I have no information."

A series of thumps and slams hit the wall, a couple with bone crunching sounds accompanying them. The man sobbed and pleaded and begged, and Ana had to curl up in Maddoc's arms, gripping his tunic so she wouldn't cry. She hated listening to all that pain and violence. How could they do it?

Just as Maddoc was placing her down so Raine could take her away, the door opened, and more footsteps came in.

"No!" the prisoner cried out. "Leave him, please!"

"I remember when you didn't pay your taxes a couple of years ago, and your grandchild was invited for the fun. You managed to find the money pretty quickly," one of the men said. "So let's see if he is as effective to get us results this time. After all, Duke Ryden is all about results."

Ana froze, but Maddoc was ushering her out of the room with Raine. Ryden? Was he was alive?

Before she had time to think about it, Raine was leading her down the steps and out onto the side road.

"I need to go back in," she urged. "I need to know if Ryden is still alive."

Raine shook her head. "Impossible."

Ana yanked her hand away. "It may be impossible for you, but I want to go back in."

Raine stared at her. "You want to go back in and see what they do to his grandchild?"

"I need to know if Ryden is still alive."

"What difference does it make if he is?" she said, disgust in her voice. "He is part of that house. He is condoning that behavior."

"You don't know that," Ana said immediately. "He may not know what they're doing in his name." Even though Aldous was an Alpha Ryden looked up to, it didn't mean Ryden was aware of this. He wasn't a representative of the house. He could be kept out of the truly terrible acts. Besides, it was too hard to believe that Ryden would know about this and approve it.

"Look," Raine said, her voice softening. "I cannot take you back in. It's already too late. Maddoc has already entered the room or kicked down the wall or something, and there were king's guard in that room. It's not just fighting knights from the houses or inexperienced men who haven't faced battle before. The king's guard are dangerous to us. They have killed many of us. I cannot take you back up there to be hurt, or taken, or distract Maddoc from what he's doing."

Ana's heart sank. She was right. Glancing back up at the house, she nodded and they both headed down the street.

❖

That evening Maddoc did not come.

Ana paced the pavilion after sundown, expecting him to enter at any moment, but when an hour passed, she began to worry that he may have really been hurt. What if Aldous had caught him, did that mean that they were coming to the camp to get Ana? What hope did the rest of the people here have without Maddoc?

She shook her head pushing away her fears. Slowing her pace down in the middle of her room, she realized that she was fearful *for* him. She didn't want anything to happen to him, and she could not go to sleep until she saw him.

Peeking out the entrance of the tent, she looked to see if anyone was nearby. Her guard stood a few feet away, but he seemed to be watching something on the other side of the camp.

She tiptoed over to him. "Do you know where Maddoc is?"

He turned, his eyes glistening in the fire light. "Yes. He will come and see you when he is ready, Princess."

"Where is he?"

The guard was silent for a moment. "He would prefer if you waited for him."

"I don't give a fuck what he prefers," she hissed. "I want to know where he is right now."

The guard eyed her. "He is in the healing tent."

“Where is that?”

The guard pointed.

"Is he all right?"

The guard didn't answer. "That's all I know." The guard's answer was noncommittal, but there was clear worry on his face, and she realized that he had been staring across at the healing tent when she approached.

Without saying another word, she walked in that direction, preparing for him to try to stop her. But he didn't, and when she glanced over her shoulder, he was simply following, escorting her there.

The healing tent was surrounded mostly in darkness, but since Ana had never been there before, she was unsure what she would find. Who was the healer in the camp? Did each camp have one or was it one for the whole base?

She stepped toward the opening and peeked inside to see Maddoc's huge form lying on a raised platform in the middle. It looked like a mix between a table and a bed, possibly what they might use in treatment rooms to treat patients. Next to the table was... Raine.

What? Ana blinked.

They were talking, and she was pressing something on Maddoc's shoulder, leaning over him and laughing as she did so.

A flare of anger sparked a growly rumble at the back of her throat. What was she doing?

"Princess, I think you should leave him to—"

"Go back to your station," Ana hissed at the guard, her anger heightening.

He stilled, then took a few steps back, but went no farther.

Ana turned back to the tent, incensed that Raine was in there. Was this really a healing tent or a fuck tent? She'd always been aware that there were probably a lot of women that Maddoc had slept with, but she'd assumed that they would be whores or disposable liaisons, much like the way he treated her—only interested in sex with her because she was an Omega and a princess, but this woman was a fucking highcloak. She was permanently by his side in battles, and he trusted her to bring the stolen Omega back to camp every day.

She scowled as she watched them. Maddoc was naked from the waist up and they talked to each other comfortably, as if nakedness wasn't a problem. The woman even brushed her hand over his skin and barely looked at him, as though she had seen him naked plenty of times before.

The more she watched, the more she disliked what was happening, and emotions rose that she didn't understand. She tried to turn away, but couldn't. She had to know what this woman was doing with her Alpha. Was she who he was with every night after he kissed her and left her?

She leaned in closer, her hands gripping the opening of the tent as the woman went around the table and rinsed a cloth in a basin nearby and then returned to place the cloth over his shoulder. Blood dripped down his arm and onto the ground, but he didn't even wince. Raine looked down at the rest of his body and murmured something, then giggled.

And that was breaking point.

All the rough, ragged feelings building in Ana took hold of her, reaching a scalding tipping point that pushed reason far from her mind. Instincts urging her forward, screaming for her to do something about this threat. And as much as Ana had not wanted to address any feelings for this Alpha, she had no choice now. She had to act.

Embracing the inner haze of fury that swept her, she stepped into the tent.

EIGHT

MADDOC

Maddoc growled at the pain that tore at his shoulder. He had been stabbed with a sword before, but didn’t recall it being so painful. It was always a risk fighting the king's guard, but he had been trained better than them, and so had most of his highcloaks. This injury happened by accident on the part of his attacker—he got lucky. It was unfortunate for him he was no longer alive to brag about it.

He groaned again. It was as though his shoulder was being trampled every time he moved, and while Raine was doing her best, he had the feeling she wasn't saying something. "What is it?" he finally growled.

Her mouth twisted as she looked at her chart and then dripped two drops of a foul-smelling liquid into the wound. "You are lucky. The sword went through the joint. It didn't hit anything major that will cause any difficulty in your arm."

"But?" Maddoc sensed something coming.

"You've lost a lot of blood, and from the way in which the skin is reacting around the wound, the sword may have been poisoned."

Maddoc was quiet for a moment. That was bad. "Do you know which one? There are antidotes to many of the poisons available."

Raine nodded. "I think so, but it would be difficult to determine, and I don't know how long this one will take." Her voice lowered. "We need our healer, Maddoc."

"We cannot use her right now. She trained you for a reason."

"Yes, but I'm not an expert with this! Your life is too important for me to guess, Maddoc."

Maddoc said nothing. He simply stared at her until she calmed down. Raine managed to control her outbursts most of the time now. "How has escorting Ana been?"

Raine made a face. "You want to talk about that now?"

"You know why I gave you that task, don't you?"

She sighed. "Yes."

"Has it helped?"

Raine shrugged while mixing some of the ingredients into a paste. "A bit. I'm trying to find the right time to talk to her."

"My experience is that there is never a right time. You just pick one and make it work."

Raine snorted. "That might work for you; she's weak for you."

Maddoc smiled at that.

"But it wouldn't work for me. She practically screamed at me to take her back into the house today."

"Why?"

Raine suddenly stilled, as though realizing she said something she shouldn't have and was backed into a corner. "She wanted to know if her betrothed is still alive," she said finally.

Maddoc growled. Ana was still concerned about him?

"It's been a lot on her to take in, Maddoc," Raine said after he'd been growling for a few long moments. "The people she thought were good people have turned out to be the opposite. I understand that she wants to know if—"

Maddoc served her a look that made her stop speaking. All the progress he thought he'd been making with Ana was now in question, all the nights he'd spent apart from her, all the times she'd looked at him without the hatred in her eyes. That had been fucking progress. He didn't like senseless killing, but finding a way to kill that fucking duke was making a lot of sense right now.

Raine sighed as though she could sense his murderous thoughts and went to rinse out the cloth in the basin. She returned and dabbed it into his shoulder. "The good thing is, if the poison is what I think it is, we have a bit of time," Raine commented. "If it had hit any major organs, we would have needed to do something quickly." She glanced down at his body. "It's pretty lucky he got you here. It's not as though there isn't enough of you to get." She laughed at her own joke, but Maddoc said nothing.

Even a lucky shot was bad if it was poisoned. He trusted Raine to patch him up and even trusted her analysis, but it might really need their healer to return to be on the cautious—

A presence in the tent made him tense. He looked over at the entrance, and at the same time, the most wonderful scent reached him, beautifully raw and so erotically sweet it made his cock hard instantly. Ana was here.

She stood just inside the entrance, her jaw clenched, glaring at both Maddoc and Raine.

"Analisa." He was about to order her back to the pavilion, but something shining in her eyes and a slight heady bitterness in her scent made him stop. He frowned at her, noticing that her gaze was locked onto Raine. Glancing at Raine, he saw she already had her palms up and was backing away from the table slowly. The women's gazes were locked onto each other.

He glanced back to examine Ana and realized she was furious. The hardness of her gaze suggested she wanted to rip Raine to pieces—but what had Raine done? She hadn't mentioned anything happening when she escorted her.

"What is it, Analisa? he asked. She didn't answer.

As Ana came farther into the tent, the more Raine slowly backed away, and Ana's scent was so powerful, it swamped the tent. The power of bitterness within it, the aggression that dominated it, shocked Maddoc. His sweet Ana, mild and unassuming, was bitterly angry about something that involved Raine.

And as she reached the table, Raine reached the back entrance of the tent and quietly slipped out.

Maddoc reached for Ana's cheek to console her now that Raine was gone, but the aggression had not left Ana's face or scent. She began to undress, shocking Maddoc to the core.

"What are you doing, Analisa?" he asked, his voice hoarse. If she undressed right now, revealing that incredible body of hers, he wasn't sure he could keep to his rule. His cock had been jerking wildly from the moment she stepped in.

But it seemed he didn't have a choice.

Ana climbed on top of him, naked. Maddoc's mouth watered at the sight. He rumbled with pleasure at seeing her climbing up his form, and he reached out with his good arm to squeeze her breasts.

But Ana did not stop climbing. Scooting up to his chest, and then farther up, she straddled his head, positioning her pussy over his mouth.

Maddoc groaned as her scent enveloped him. He never thought she could smell any better, but this rich, luxurious aroma was beyond any experience of her he'd had. He undid his pants to give his cock relief and then grabbed her hips and pulled her pussy down onto his mouth, suckling on her lips and her clit and licking everything he could reach. But then she moved again.

Wriggling on top of him while he tried to tongue her, she moved farther up and he took the opportunity to bite her ass cheeks and wriggled his tongue over each perfect round cheek and everything he could reach. Ana wriggled her hips above him in the sexiest way, and he couldn't help but groan, then she wriggled back down to his mouth where he latched onto her clit and began to work it gently with his mouth. The moans coming from her throat made his cock leak, but nothing prepared him for the sight of her above him, her swaying breasts, the bliss of surrender on her face coupled with a fierceness in her eyes that made him want to fuck her raw. She gripped his hair as she rode his mouth, her hips writhing and jerking as she sought her release.

Maddoc had never seen anything sexier. He loved dominating Ana, truly brutally using her body and feeling her accept him the way that he knew she loved, but something about this drew on an instinctual need that satisfied him more. He couldn't understand it yet, but right now, he didn't need to.

Her climax wrecked her body, jerking her hips harder against him, blasting screams from her throat, and spasming her right leg. She dug her hands into his scalp as her pussy gushed its succulent sweet release, and when her clit's throbbing on his tongue began to wane, she moved off his mouth and wriggled downward. Her knee pressed close to the wound on his shoulder, but he ignored the pain as he watched his Omega scoot down his chest to get more of what she needed. A trail of her fluids smeared his chest, and suddenly he realized what she was doing.

His Omega had been claiming him in the most animalistic way. She'd rubbed her pussy all over his face and his chest to mark him with her most intimate of fluids to warn off other women—namely Raine.

He didn't know why she thought Raine was a threat—he would have laughed out loud if he wasn't so intensely aroused.

Ana might not be talking to him, she might fight him and resist their attraction, and even deny everything he says, but her most basic instincts told her to take steps to claim him in a way that he could never have anticipated. And when she sank herself onto his cock, her tight, wet channel drawing him in so beautifully, there was nothing that could stop him from lifting off the bed and fucking her the way she deserved.

Their mating was loud and rough and raw, the grunts, panting, and yells from both of them filling the entire tent as she rode him on her toes, her slick squirting all over him, the bed, the floor as she took his cock. Maddoc squeezed her neck with one hand, and grabbed her hip with the other, fucking her down onto him with all the force he could manage. When her back arched, he flicked her nipple with his tongue, and nibbled and bit until her guttural moans were yelps. She braced herself with a hand on his wounded shoulder, her nails digging into the wounded muscle.

The pain had no impact on the savagery of their mating. Both of them instinctively understanding the need for all potential threats to be eliminated. For Maddoc, a kindling of hope bloomed in his chest that Ana would come around to understanding what they mean to each other. He had never heard of Omegas doing anything like what she had done, but it was clear why she did it. The entire tent now smelled of her, of them, and no scent of Raine remained. And he was getting the fuck of his life.

When she orgasmed again, he bit down harder on her nipples and twisted her hips as he pummeled her, each soaking slam equally as loud as her screams. He took all the pleasure he could from watching her body, and he lifted up and she tilted into another orgasm straightaway. The pain in his shoulder tried to get his attention, but he was too busy watching his Omega as she climbed another peak, soaring, the most beautiful expression on her face.

His orgasm was the strongest he'd ever had. Grabbing her ass, she slammed down on him, once, twice, three times as her groans became raspy and gruff, and he bellowed as his knot smashed in stretching her clenching pussy wide, connecting them in a way that only an Alpha and Omega could.

He held her in his arms as they both panted, contentment blending with his lingering orgasm as his Omega lay limp and exhausted in his arms.

Maddoc watched her fall asleep. She couldn't deny it now; she belonged to him, and she wanted him to belong to her. It didn't matter what she said or did, she had just taken steps to claim him, and she couldn't explain away that behavior.

So when she woke, it was time to discuss his real plans with her, and she would talk to him, whether she liked it or not.

❖

The next morning, as Ana stirred awake, Maddoc pulled her tight against him and kissed her deeply.

She responded slowly, threading her hands through his hair and sucking on his tongue, a whimper on her breath as their mouths locked.

He pulled away and looked down at her. "Good morning, Analisa."

She stared at him for a long moment, an unreadable expression on her face. Her eyes were different now. There was no defiance in them. No fire or hardness. Something had certainly changed, but if it didn't produce a different result, then it remained unacceptable.

Maddoc tugged at her chin until she looked back at him, a hard edge in his voice when he spoke again. “I said, good morning.”

Various expressions flitted across Ana’s face that Maddoc couldn’t decipher, but she remained silent.

He growled, sitting up and yanking her up with him. He pulled her into his lap and looked her in the eye. "Do you know what you did yesterday?"

She nodded, her eyes lowering, face glum.

“And you are still choosing not to speak?” Maddoc exhaled harshly, grabbing her and pulling her closer. "You cannot have it both ways, Ana. You cannot rub your pussy all over me to warn off other females and then be unwilling to talk to me! How long do you think I will allow this?” He grabbed the back of her head and yanked her back. “Do I really need to fuck other women until you admit it?”

Ana’s mouth trembled, but she didn’t move or answer.

"Answer me! How can you continue with this behavior after yesterday?"

Finally, her eyes rose and met his, but they were filled with tears. "You killed him."

Conflicting emotions spiraled in Maddoc’s chest, both tempering each other, both bringing about a realization that he did not want to accept. "Your father was deeply involved in every atrocity you have witnessed in the last four days, and many *many* more you haven’t."

She nodded, tears spilling onto her cheeks. "But he was still my father."

Maddoc growled and released her. "So you will allow his crimes and keep a false memory of him to mourn, but you will not accept what is real between you and me?"

Ana shook her head. "It's not that." She slid off his lap and sat cross-legged on the bed. Maddoc forced himself not to drag her back, if only so she would speak. "I can't deny anything you've said," she said miserably. "I can't explain what is happening between us. All I know is that I feel and behave differently with you. I am… confused by it. It doesn't fit with anything I know or recognize. But that's not the only confusing thing. *Everything* is different now. My life, the life I knew, has been so distorted by what you've shown me… I don't know how to view it anymore. What is my life supposed to be?"

"Your life is with me, Ana."

"Is it?" She shrugged, pulling her knees up and hugging them. "How do I know? For years, I thought it was with Ryden. Since I was born, I thought it was the court. I thought my life would follow the footsteps of my father. Now you are saying it is with you, when the first thing you did was use and humiliate me, then you hurt the people I care about, and now you keep me here."

"You were never used," Maddoc said sharply. "You were reporting to your parents. There were things I couldn't say, and you wouldn't have believed me anyway. It may seem harsh, but certain things had to happen, Ana."

"Like Milly's home being attacked? Her husband being killed?"

Maddoc scowled and got up from the bed.

"That was when I decided I couldn't trust you," she said quietly. "When I realized you willingly hurt innocent people to punish others."

"You still think they are all innocent?" Maddoc bellowed, anger blazing in his chest. "Even now? Milly's husband knew what would come eventually, Ana. All of them do. That is why they are so afraid of me."

A frown flickered across her face, but he continued.

"You are here because this is where you belong. Do you think you can somehow go back to the court and play princess again? Do you intend to take your place among murderers, thieves, and rapists? Is that why you yearn for that fucking duke?"

"No," she shot back. "I do not. But I also don't want to be here watching young children like Trea grow up to kill, to see this never-ending cycle of killing and abuse. All that bright light in her will be put out if she has to witness those things."

Maddoc was silent for a moment. "That will not happen. Trea will never be a highcloak, none of the children here will. This will not be a generational fight, Ana. That's not the plan."

"Then what *is* the plan?" she cried. "You are the only one who knows it. Am I supposed to live here in the middle of the Oakenshire while you and your men save some of the commoners from the houses? What about the rest of them? The Allandis people are supposed to be *my* responsibility." Ana pushed herself up to her knees, her voice breaking. "Do you know how hard it is to see those crimes happening to them? That is not what the crown was supposed to be about, it's not what the royal houses were supposed to be about. All my studies and training have been *against* this, my father was against this. And without him, I don't know why it happened or how to correct it." She shook her head, closing her eyes and holding in the sobs that threatened. "I made a promise to myself to still be a princess to those people," she whispered, "to uphold everything the crown stood for. It was the only thing that helped me get out of bed when I first got here." She opened her eyes. "I have no purpose anymore. So if you want me to be your little pet Omega, to take your cock and tell you pretty things, and do whatever you say, I'll do that. I'll be anything you want me to be. But I'm still my father's daughter, and you killed him."

Sobbing, she lowered onto the bed, curling herself into a ball.

Maddoc held back from comforting her, the sinking feeling in his stomach tingling around his whole body. He had done this all wrong.

When they didn't have their third night together, too many things changed from his original plan. He had overwhelmed her with the wrong information, and now she couldn't even see the way forward, or that her way forward was with him. He'd been relying on her to trust her instincts, but she never would, because she'd been cocooned in an environment that taught her not to. The same environment that taught her never to trust him or anything he said.

He needed to correct that, and he needed to do it in a way she understood.

Clenching his jaw, he turned to the entrance of his pavilion. "Tonight, you will go home."

Eight

NINE

ANA

Maddoc didn't return until just before dusk. He entered with a bundle of furs and hats and cloaks and threw them down on the table before pulling her out of bed to dress her. Ana observed him. He seemed solemn as he untangled her hair, but she couldn't judge his mood.

She'd spent the day in bed, mulling over their conversation and everything that happened since she arrived, but she still couldn't make sense of much. Part of her recognized she was exhausted and emotionally drained and couldn't think clearly about anything. It could be what happened yesterday in the healing tent, or it could be the breaking point of seeing all that abuse in the kingdom. Another part of her recognized that she had stopped thinking of trying to escape—that she was starting to care Maddoc was successful when they went out to interfere with the royal houses. And that scared her. She could see with her own eyes that what the houses were doing was wrong, but after reading all those reports and hearing about Maddoc's "destruction" all her life, supporting him felt like treason. Not to mention, she was beginning to care greatly for *him* beyond their attraction.

"Why do you always dress me every morning," she asked tentatively.

Maddoc made a sound in the back of his throat. "It is not morning."

Ana lowered her head. So he was still annoyed.

After a moment, he said, "I started doing it because it was the only way I could have time with you alone when I stopped sleeping in here. And then I noticed you enjoyed it, so I kept doing it."

A flush crept up Ana's neck. She did enjoy it, and it was for the same reason—she wanted to be near him.

"I need to bathe," she said, as he pulled on a thick tunic over her head.

"No."

"But… I smell."

Maddoc paused, looking at her in the eyes. "Should *I* bathe?"

Ana leaned forward to sniff him. He still smelled of last night, and it wasn't just her scent—her dried, old slick still coated his face and neck. Her cheeks burned with embarrassment as she leaned back, but deep within her, a preening satisfaction bloomed that he smelled like he was hers.

"Should I?" he asked again.

Ana shook her head.

Maddoc dipped his head in agreement. "And neither will you. You will smell of me while you travel so all are aware. Bathe when you get there."

"Get where?" His cryptic last line to her earlier seemed to suggest he would take her back to the palace, but she knew that wasn't the case. She wasn't even sure she wanted to go back.

Maddoc didn't answer. Once she was wrapped in layers of clothing and furs, he lifted her into his arms. They trudged outside as the darkening skies approached, and when they reached the campfire several families stood with the highcloaks, talking excitedly among themselves.

"These families are coming with us?" Ana asked, confused.

Maddoc nodded.

They exited the camp and traveled through the dense trees as usual, but when they got to the more spacious area, no horses waited. They trudged through the forest on foot, veering sharply to the right, and the whole party was quiet, even the children. Ana noticed that Maddoc was carrying her slightly differently, more heavily on his left arm.

"I can walk if your shoulder hurts," she said, quietly.

"No."

"If we walk for too long, your injury could get worse," she insisted.

"It's not much longer."

"Did…" Ana swallowed. "Did Raine finish treating it?"

"No, but there's not much she can do anyway."

"What do you mean." Ana's voice rose slightly, a tinge of panic fluttering in her chest.

Maddoc glanced at her, his beard twitching. "Our main healer is traveling, but I will see her to treat me."

Ana relaxed a little. "Oh."

After a while, they came to a wide river. Ana looked up and down it curiously. This must be the river Joe and Conrad's camp had been talking about. It was calm, not a ripple across the waters reflecting the fading sun.

Maddoc carefully set Ana down and drew something from his pocket. The families around whispered quietly, eager for something, everyone watching Maddoc and the river.

He held a fist of what looked like sparkling sand over the water and sprinkled it in a circular motion until his hand was empty. The sand made tiny, golden, ripples in the waves, and as Ana watched them, they came together and hardened to form a huge, flat, golden raft with tiny ridges on its top.

Ana opened her mouth and then closed it again, blinking to make sure she hadn't just seen the impossible. The sand suddenly turned into the raft? But before she could say anything, the families and highcloaks were already climbing on.

Ana dragged her eyes from the raft, her eyes wide on Maddoc. "Did you do that?" she gasped.

Maddoc chuckled.

Ana's eyes widened even further and she turned to look back at the raft. "That's magic?"

"Yes."

Ana stared at the raft as the families all climbed on and shuffled near the middle. The highcloaks stood around the edges.

Maddoc took Ana's head in his hands and pulled her eyes back to him. "Analisa." Ana quickly sobered, at the strange look in his eyes. "It was not my intention to shoot your father." His low voice rumbled through her just as it always did when he spoke quietly close to her. "I did what I had to do in battle, and in that one, I took actions against the man who ripped my Omega from my arms. I didn't know it was your father until my arrow released from my bow."

Ana swallowed, recalling how quick everything happened.

"I do not regret shooting him," he clarified, "but I am sorry that you are unable to see past your grief for such a man. Your father made an agreement with me that he would let me keep you if I got to you first. And I did. But he still tried to take you away."

Ana opened her mouth to say something but nothing came out. What could she say? Why would her father make such an agreement? She recognized that there was very little point in Maddoc lying about it, but Father was also not here to defend himself.

"I know you are already forming excuses for him in your mind," Maddoc said, a snarl in his throat. "You are a specialist at making excuses for them."

Ana smiled at him, but it was sad. "We come from very different worlds, Maddoc."

"That does not mean we do not belong together," he said. "We do. Once I have finished my duties, I will join you."

Ana frowned. "What do you…?" She glanced at the raft. "You're not coming with us?"

Maddoc kissed her hard, just the way he always had when he came to see her in the evenings, full of passion and longing and a desperate need to taste her. When he pulled away Ana had tears in her eyes, but she didn't know why. "I thought you were coming with us," she said accusingly.

"Griff will look after you," Maddoc said, ignoring her. "Unfortunately, he is an Alpha and also a male. So I will not permit him to stand near you."

Ana snorted softly.

"You may send messages to him through a female."

At that she did laugh, and Maddoc's eyes softened. "I will see you soon, my Analisa."

He let go of her and suddenly she felt unsteady without him. She wasn't ready to step away.

"Princess," one of the high cloaks called. "You can step on, it's safe."

Ana turned. Everyone was waiting for her, but she hesitated. Finally, Maddoc lifted her and placed her on the raft. As soon as he let her go, it began to move smoothly and swiftly across the river.

"Wait!" She turned to Maddoc, but he was already shrinking into the distance. Tears sprang to her eyes as desperation and panic began to overwhelm her.

"Princess Ana!"

Ana turned to see Alice standing on the raft, Trea on her hip. "Alice? I didn't realize you were here."

Before Alice could respond, Trea reached for Ana, climbing into her arms. She wrapped her arms around Ana's neck and her legs around Ana's torso.

Ana laughed and patted her back. "Are you scared of the raft, Trea?"

"No, I'm protecting you," she said into her neck.

"You are?" Ana said, smiling at Alice.

"Yes," she said. "Doc said it's my first mission."

Ana's face dropped. She turned to look back at Maddoc but she could no longer see him. She blinked away tears that rose as Alice placed a hand on her arm.

"He'll be with us again before you even know it," she said gently.

The raft moved along the river at an unnatural speed. The river barely rippled as it slid along the water. Trea encouraged Ana to sit with them among the families. The little girl wanted snacks while completing her mission, then she promptly fell asleep. Ana rocked her gently and kept glancing back in the direction they'd come, wondering how far they were going.

When she turned to look ahead, she noticed the river opening up to a wide lake or sea, but she wasn't aware of anything like that in the Oakenshire. However, Allandis was enormous, and some of it remained unexplored. Maddoc had said he had traveled all of it, and at this point she was willing to believe she was heading somewhere safe.

"Do you know where we're going?" she asked Alice.

"Not exactly," Alice said, her eyes were alive with excitement. "But I can't wait to get there. Trea and I are the first coming here from our camp."

"The rest of the camp is coming?"

Alice nodded.

Within a quarter of an hour, it looked like land was rising up on the horizon, coming toward them quickly as the raft sped forward. The families around her jittered in excitement, but Ana was nervous. She had never left the known areas of Allandis before, and now she suddenly realized, she was without the one person who always managed to calm her. She glanced up at the highcloaks and Griff was looking back at her. He nodded in reassurance. She forced herself to relax.

She watched the land come closer, hills and buildings coming into view as they neared.

Within another quarter of an hour, they were slowing as they neared the beach. The raft headed right into the beach and then jolted as it landed on the sand, dissolving itself and causing the passengers to fall over each other.

Trea laughed heartily and Ana found herself laughing with her as she got up and brushed the sand from her clothes.

The beach spread as far as the eye could see in both directions, but behind them were beautiful, well-kept gardens.

"We're going this way, Princess," Griff called, heading towards the gardens.

She turned to see that the families and some of the other highcloaks were heading in a different direction. Alice waved at her, but Trea hadn't yet noticed that Ana was not with them, so she quickly tiptoed away with the highcloaks.

Griff led the way, but it wasn't until she was halfway across the gardens that she realized five other highcloaks surrounded her in a wide circumference. One of them was Raine.

Ana stared at her, wondering why she didn't feel any anger toward her now, but it had been so intense then. Maddoc never confirmed or denied if anything happen between them. It was something she should have asked.

As they veered around the gardens, a magnificent building came into view. Ana abruptly stopped.

"Who lives there?" she asked, astonished. She'd never seen any building styled in such a way. Cream and gold made up the whole multistory building, and shimmery gold paneling decorated some of the walls around enormous arched windows, and thick towers reached to the sky topped with round spheres and spires. It was expansive, but beautifully balanced with balconies, shrubs, and large trees with wide flat leaves. Ana couldn't help but gape. She couldn't still be in Allandis; she would have known if this building existed within her kingdom. They had to have traveled to a different kingdom.

"We need to keep going, Your Majesty," Griff said. "We must reach the palace before dusk."

Ana's brows lifted. Palace? Yes, that suited it.

They kept walking until they reached the building, and although there were guards standing around the building, the highcloaks led her straight in through the front. It was even more impressive than the outside. Simple furniture, simple colors, and without the clutter and heavy ornamentation of the palace that she called home. It was beautiful.

"Ana!"

The familiar voice that rang out in the entrance hall made her freeze. "Milly?"

Milly ran to her, throwing her arms around her and hugging her tight.

"Milly! What are you doing here?" Milly's familiar smell drew on all the memories she had of her home, her bedchamber, her library, her studies, her life at the palace. Milly signified everyday life, and the familiarity of it made Ana tearful yet again.

"We've been waiting for you," Milly said pulling back to her arm's length, tears in her own eyes.

"What do you mean?" Ana looked around the palace. "Who is we? And how long have you been here?"

"Not that long, but you were supposed to be here already, from what I was told." She scowled. "It's so difficult to get anything from any of these guards."

Ana blinked slowly, nothing made sense. "I don't understand."

"Let's get you settled and then we can talk."

Milly led her through a number of corridors to an elegant living space with a light airy feel to it, even as the skies were darkening outside. Ana stared out the window and saw the skies had a tinge of pink to them that she hadn't seen before. When they'd left Maddoc in the Oakenshire, dusk had already arrived. "Where are we, Milly?"

Milly grinned. "In Allandis. Can you believe it?"

"No. I don't understand how."

Milly patted the sofa next to her. "I have only been here a few days myself," she admitted. "But from what I understand, all this belongs to Maddoc."

Ana made a face, holding up her hand in confusion. "Wait, tell me how you got here first."

"After I spoke to you when my husband died—" She swallowed a sip of wine. "—I was approached by one of the courtiers in the palace. He said he had a job for me doing something similar to what I did now, but that it would take me away from the palace and my life, and everything that I'd known."

"And you just believed it?" Ana asked in disbelief.

"No, no of course not. But then," Milly's voice lowered, and her shoulders dropped. "My son recovered from the attack, but he was very bitter and angry about everything. He refused to get a job or even think about a trade, and I could tell he didn't want me around while he tried to correct his own life. I really had no reason to stay in Allandis. I wouldn't have been able to keep my job with you without some kind of status from my son in his work. And someone was offering me similar work, better pay, living accommodation… It was very tempting," she said lifting her shoulders. "And then, with the attack of the king at your wedding, I just didn't want to be in the palace anymore. The kingdom was going to suffer, and I didn't want to live a life with no status." She leaned forward. "I know it sounds bad, but when you have no status, things can be very bad for you."

Ana wondered if she knew. "Did you know about the corruption of the royal houses?"

""No," Milly said sharply. "I never knew until I accepted this job. I was given a study with books and reports to create my lessons on, and some of those books had information in them that shocked me. Names, dates, places, written accounts…" Her mouth became a thin line and her chin trembled as she stared at Ana. "I never would have stayed there if I had known. I even found out that my husband had been involved in…" She lowered her head and swallowed. "I cannot bear to think about their actions."

She looked down at her hand for a long moment, to the place her wedding ring used to be. "I'm not saying I don't miss him dearly, but I won't excuse him. Edward knew right from wrong. I cannot understand what compelled him. Now that I lost my status, something like that could have happened to me. And you know I did not tolerate those gossips in the Royal Court, so they could have targeted me very easily."

Ana nodded thoughtfully. Milly did not make excuses for her husband's behavior the way Maddoc said she made excuses for her father. "But…" Ana stared at Milly. "How are you all right with this? How are you comfortable with Maddoc? After everything that has been said about him."

"Well, I haven't met him yet," Milly said. "I'm sure I will not be comfortable, in fact, I'll be terrified. But once I knew about the royal houses, I had to decide which was worse. And if what they said about him wasn't true, then I don't really know him at all. Also, after what happened at your wedding, I suspected that you would be here. And I was willing to risk it to see you again." She smiled.

Ana exhaled a breath and thought about what she said. "So you're giving him a clean slate?"

"No, not exactly," Milly said. "But I could no longer trust what we've been told about him, and I was desperate to leave. It is a risk."

"Milly," Ana said, carefully "Do you think Father was involved? I find it difficult to believe he was. You spoke to my parents regularly and you saw them together…. Do you think they were allowing these atrocities to happen?"

Milly leaned back in the chair. "I don't know. Everything in me tells me that they did not, and I cannot believe that I would be that wrong about them."

Ana held her breath, knowing more was coming.

"But if that is the case, I cannot see how it could have gotten so bad with the houses." She shook her head. "That they were doing things out in the open, where anyone could have seen them. They were so bold in their abuse, and that usually comes from having some kind of power that is impossible to overcome." She snorted. "If your father had been healed enough before I left, I would have questioned him within an inch of his life."

Ana sat up straight, her stomach twisting. "What did you say?"

"I would have interrogated your father thoroughly before I left, if he had been up to it." Milly looked furious. "Even if he had nothing to do with what the royal houses were doing, it still happened during his reign. He is supposed to protect the commoners! There's no excuse for being unaware of what is happening to his people."

"He's alive?" Ana slowly rose from her seat, amazement threading through her and fogging up her throat. "Father is alive?"

Milly's eyes widened. "You were not told? Yes! Your father is alive, Ana!"

"How could I be told?" Ana cried. "I've been with Maddoc since the wedding, I've had no news."

Milly frowned. "But he is alive because of Maddoc, from what I have heard." She looked around the room, as if searching for something or someone to clarify, but there was no one else in the room but them.

"What do you mean?"

"Well… that's what I was told."

Ana sat next to her. "How is he? Can you tell me how he's doing?"

Milly patted the back of her hand. "That is all I know," she said apologetically.

Ana exhaled, a bubble of relief and astonishment buoyant in her chest. If Father was alive, that put so much hope back into her heart about the possibilities for the kingdom. “Do you know how the royals are taking it?”

“From what I hear, there has already been three assassination attempts,” Milly said gravely. “I anticipate that they will eventually succeed, if he doesn’t recover quickly enough to do something about it. Ryden is currently acting king, regent king, while your father is sick, but only until they find you.”

Ana breathed hard, her mind trying to process all of the information at once. Ryden was alive too. And he was currently king, just like he always wanted! All it would take would be for her to go back to the kingdom and enforce her right as heir, and they would rule while Father recovered.

Everything would be how it was, and between them they could correct the corruption the houses were causing. But if that was a worthwhile plan, why didn’t she feel more excited about the idea.

“I can see you have plenty of things to think about,” Milly said, quietly.

Ana nodded. She didn’t have to ask Milly if she would ever go back, she knew she wouldn’t. Milly was much firmer than Ana, and her assessment of the courts, and of Maddoc, was more logical than Ana’s. And it made her feel like an ignorant child, once again.

“In the meantime,” Milly said, a smile spreading on her face as she lifted her arms and spread them around the room. “You should explore.”

❖

It was strange walking around the palace. Although everything about it screamed wealth, it didn’t look the way she knew wealth looked. There were definite similarities, but this one had an exotic feel to it, as though created by a long-forgotten culture. It's beauty was in its simplicity and fine details, and that was what made Ana begin to fall in love with it. If Maddoc wanted this to be her home, he'd certainly made a good effort.

On the ground floor, she opened a set of double doors with distinctive engravings over the panels to find an enormous library.

She rushed inside and spun in a circle, squealing, looking at everything, but heading over to examine the shelves. It was the biggest collection of books and parchment she'd ever seen, and excitement rose in her at the idea that new books were waiting for her to explore.

Upstairs in the bedroom, there was an enormous wardrobe tucked into the wall with extravagant dresses, including the two he had ripped off her those two nights. They'd both been repaired so well, it was as though they had never been torn.

When she turned to the bed, a familiar book lay on it, and Ana laughed as she picked it up. It was her favorite book, the one she brought to the room the first night she saw Maddoc. She never thought she would see it again.

She entered each of her private rooms, filled with excitement about the beauty of what she was seeing and enjoying the reminders of her Alpha. The enormous washroom had a bath so big, it favored a small lake. Handmaids drew her a bath and scented her water with oils, and she took her time washing, savoring the feel of the comfort she had once been so used to.

When she headed to bed, Milly popped in, and they sat talking about everything that happened since they'd been apart. Ana told her about the agreement she'd almost made with some of the houses, much to Milly's horror, and Milly explained to her that beyond the palace there was a city that was just as beautiful and as strange as the palace. Ana wondered about where the families from Moonvale had gone, and she hoped they were enjoying wherever they were. She made a note to ask the highcloaks.

Climbing into bed, Ana realized there was no Alpha to hold her and no scent to comfort her in her sleep. Luckily, she was exhausted by the time her head hit the pillow and she fell asleep straightaway.

The next day she spent hours in the library looking over all the shelves and getting familiar with as many books as she could so she could try to find the next great read. Amazingly, there was an entire wall dedicated to Alpha and Omega stories, copies of all the stories and retelling she'd seen in her library and many more.

She began reading some of the Alpha and Omega stories that she hadn't seen before, some of them dating back before Allandis existed. One of them even chronicled the story of King Allandis, the Alpha who founded the kingdom, and his haphazard, misfit Omega, Elyana.

Ana spent nearly three days buried in books covering the Alpha and Omega couples of Allandis, and the more she read, the more she understood her attraction to Maddoc. Much of the feelings described—

intoxicating, addictive, a satisfying sense of completion—were how she would describe the many times she'd been with him. And it was through those emotions that she could understand the choices the couples made for the kingdom and why they made them. *That must be how an Alpha and Omega rule*—how her parents made their decisions. But that thought raised more questions.

Ana lay in bed thinking about how similar the connection between an Alpha and an Omega was across all the stories; it was almost identical in each one. Something nudged at her to make another connection, but her mind was too sleepy, and when she woke the next morning, it was gone.

❖

On the fourth night, Ana paced the bedroom in agitation. She wanted to see Maddoc. In her rational mind, she had questions to ask him that he should have answered before he sent her here, but in her irrational mind, she just wanted to be near him, in his arms again. Not seeing him or talking to him for four days was torturous and she didn't like that she'd heard nothing about him.

Sighing, she tried to calm herself and sat on the bed cross-legged. Clearly Maddoc had a plan that included them both being here. He never mentioned it to her, but it was vastly different than what she thought he expected from her.

A knock at the door interrupted her thoughts. "Come in."

The door inched open, and Raine slipped through, pressing herself against the wall.

"I'm sorry to disturb you, Your Majesty," she said hurriedly. "I just wanted to… welcome you."

Ana smiled, trying to put her at ease. "Thank you, Raine."

Raine relaxed a tiny amount. "I just wanted to welcome you and say that…" She fidgeted. "I hope we can, at some point, be friends."

Ana suddenly noticed Raine was not dressed as a highcloak. She wore a tunic with pants and a belt around her waist. Ana examined her, trying to figure out why she'd had hostile feelings toward her. Raine had never been aggressive or unfriendly toward Ana. In fact, she had been always polite and cordial. Her disheveled auburn hair that was usually tied back into one plait, fell to her shoulders and she was very pretty, just very different from Ana. Ana hadn't noticed any attraction or a suggestion of such between Raine and Maddoc in all the time they were traveling into Allandis.

"I don't know what I may have done to upset you." She looked crestfallen. "But we… I've looked forward to you being with us for a long time. I hope that someday you will come to trust me as a highcloak or at least as a guard. Maddoc will never let me near you if he thinks you'll be upset. He wouldn't let me treat him after… what happened."

Ana scowled. Maddoc wouldn't let her treat him? He had not made that clear. "You didn't do anything to upset me, Raine," she said, eager to put her at ease. "I don't know why I reacted that way."

Raine smiled. "I think it's because you have great instincts."

"Do I?" Ana tilted her head. "Are you sexually involved with him?"

Raine's face distorted into an expression of absolute horror. "No! That's disgusting!" She quickly held a hand out. "Not meaning to offend, Your Majesty. It's just… *no.* He is like a big brother to me."

"Then my instincts are not that great at all." Ana laughed. "I've been reading some of the Alpha and Omega books and I don't know how mine could be so… wrong."

"Wrong? They're not wrong, Your Majesty. The two of you…" Raine sighed, a smile on her face. "The two of you are what gives the rest of us hope. That maybe one day we will find that."

Ana's smile faded as she recalled how often she'd nursed that hope when looking at her parents. The way her mother melted so contently into her father's lap, the way they soothed each other with their touch, the undeniable attraction—the most powerful thing in every room. She and Maddoc had that. Sometimes it was hot and tense, sometimes it was explosive and violent. But it was always there, from that very first night. She glanced up at Raine, suddenly feeling exposed. "I… I'm sorry, I just…."

Raine shrugged. "That's all right. You love him and you miss him. I understand."

Ana blinked. Did she love him?

"I've been dealing with it for five years already with him, so I'm used to it."

Ana leaned forward. "What do you mean?"

"Him pining for you." Raine grinned, jokingly rolling her eyes. "It was a hard five years. Honestly, we really are glad you're here."

"Five years?" Ana stared at her. "Maddoc has felt that way for me for five years?"

Raine froze. "I'm not sure if he would want me to tell you that." She pursed her lips and shrugged. "But it's true. Everything changed five years ago, in terms of the focus of our missions, preparing this place, and dealing with the crown. Everything became streamlined and more urgent. We didn't all know why at first, but it eventually became clear."

Ana wracked her brain trying to think what happened five years ago that Maddoc would have suddenly focused on her.

"I suggest you talk to him about it," Raine said. "I'm sure he is trying to manage the information he gives you, and I'm sure he hasn't explained himself well at all, as usual. But you should know how crazy he is about you. He talks about you all the time."

Ana recalled how friendly everyone was at Moonvale when she arrived, and Trea's insistence that she wasn't mean like other members of the court.

She exhaled, the weight of the revelation pressing heavily on her. This was… She thought for a moment. Obvious. It was obvious when looking at the facts. She'd never been attracted to Ryden, not once. The only difference between her and Maddoc and the Alpha and Omega couples from the books were that they were not fated to be together. What went so wrong with her? Could something have gone wrong with her pairing that led her to an Alpha who wasn't hers? Mother had been so insistent, so had Father. In fact, everyone had.

"I should go," Raine said, interrupting her thoughts. "I just wanted to say welcome. It's so nice to have an Omega here."

Ana straightened, something clicking into place. She looked over Raine again. Petite, shapely, and pretty. "Do you mean… nice to have *another* Omega here?"

Raine's eyes widened. "I told you your instincts were great!"

Ana laughed, but she upturned her palms in surprise. "But you don't have an Omega scent?"

Raine lifted her left wrist to show her a thin bracelet secured to it. "This prevents it," she said. "But you guessed it from that night. I don't know how."

"I don't know how, either," Ana admitted. "It was very… I never really thought about it when it was happening, and it came over me so quickly."

"It could have been heightened from your arousal or attraction and connection to Maddoc," Raine explained. "Especially if you hadn't been together much."

Ana squinted at her. "You know about Alphas and Omegas?"

"I've been trying to learn," she admitted. "But there isn't anyone I can talk to about it who understands. That's why I was hoping we could be friends."

Ana smiled at her. "Of course we can."

Raine let out a heavy breath of relief and finally pushed herself off the wall. "Good," she breathed. "I have been in some scary fights in my life as a highcloak, but I've never been as scared as when you came into that tent. Your scent was…"

Ana laughed with her, though a little awkwardly. "I'm sorry about that, it really was not intentional."

"That's all right. I suppose you are still learning how to deal with your attraction and assessing all threats. There are bound to be some hiccups. It's the same with training."

"So you are a highcloak and an Omega? I'm surprised Maddoc allowed it."

"I didn't let him tell me what to do," Raine said firmly. "I won't let anyone fight on my behalf when I can help. Some women are best at supporting by being back at base. But not me. I cannot twiddle my fingers when I'm best on the field. It took a long time for Maddoc to learn that, but he finally did."

There was so much Ana wanted to ask, but as soon as she yawned, Raine took her leave.

"We have plenty of time to talk another day," Raine insisted.

Ana smiled and wished her a good night before climbing into bed, wrestling with a number of thoughts, but too tired to make any more connections.

❖

The next morning, as she left the library, three highcloaks hurried past her with a sense of urgency, heading to the exit.

"Raine," Ana called. "What's happened?"

"We're going back to Allandis," Raine said.

The way she said it, Ana knew something was wrong. "Why?"

"Stay here and wait for us to return, Your Majesty."

"What has happened, Raine?"

When Raine stopped in the corridor and hesitated, Ana demanded. "Tell me!"

"It's Maddoc," Raine said. "He was working to bring all the people from our guild here, the ones who are part of our guild who are still in the mainland, but he's missing. It is suspected he was caught."

Ana gasped. "By who?"

Raine pressed her lips together. "The current king." She clenched her fist in frustration. "Maddoc never would have allowed himself to get into that situation, unless he was injured. His shoulder must have worsened."

"What do you mean, getting worse?" Ana asked, alarmed. "You said you didn't treat him, but I thought it wasn't that serious?"

"No, the wound in his shoulder was poisoned, Your Majesty. He needed further treatment."

"Poison?" Panic gripped Ana, and she forced herself to remember what Maddoc's words. "The healer was going to treat him. A Moonvale healer."

Raine shook her head, almost apologetically. "No, your Majesty. Our healer is with your father. Maddoc sent her to him the day he was shot. He is recovering, but it is a very slow process. She can only use a small amount of magic at a time to treat such a delicate wound. Maddoc knew she would be with him for weeks."

Ana stepped back as if she'd been struck. All this time she'd been accusing Maddoc of killing her father and he never mentioned that he was alive or that he sent his healer to treat him. Why didn't he say anything? A niggling thought at the back of her mind prodded her.

"Raine, what is taking so long." Griff strode down the corridor toward them, stopping behind Raine. "Apologies, Your Majesty, but we need to go, now."

"I'm coming with you," Ana said firmly.

Both Raine and Griff immediately said no.

"You must stay here," Griff said. "We will be back as soon as we can. There is nothing to worry about."

"If Maddoc has been captured, there is plenty to worry about," she snapped back.

Griff shot Raine a stern look.

"Don't blame her," Ana said. "I made her tell me. I want to know what is happening. You've brought me to this very strange, very different place and I've been here practically on my own when Maddoc said that he would be coming. If he is in danger, I want to help. I want to be there anyway I can."

"It will be extremely dangerous back in Allandis," Griff warned, "especially if Maddoc has been caught. Everyone will be searching for you, and if they get you, they will seek to use you to gain access to the throne, or to threaten it. It's too much of a risk."

"Not to mention that Maddoc will murder us for putting you back in danger," Raine added.

Griff looked at her, his brows raising slightly as he considered what she said. "I'm sure you know that is not an exaggeration," he said to Ana. "If you recall, the last highcloak that disobeyed his orders regarding you was shot in the leg with an arrow."

Ana clenched her fists, scowling in frustration, but Griff was firm.

"The best thing you can do is wait here," Raine said gently. "Knowing you're here, will give him more reason to fight to come back."

Ana almost growled at her. Wasn't she the one that said she didn't like sitting behind twiddling her thumbs while others risked their lives? Granted, Ana didn't have training, but she had knowledge of royal court.

"And you are not alone here, Your Majesty," Griff said. "All the families that were at Moonvale are living in the city nearby. Camp sixteen in particular has been asking to visit you, but I thought you may want some time on your own to get to know your palace and recover from what you've been through."

"The families are all here?"

Griff nodded.

"Did the assembly find Moonvale?"

"Not yet."

Ana sighed. "All right. How can I help with the families who are arriving? Are they all arriving at the beach?"

"Yes," Griff said. "They are coming from different parts of Allandis, but they will all end up at the same beach. They would be thrilled if you would greet them at their arrival. I will ask some guards to escort you."

Ana nodded. "Thank you."

Raine stepped forward and grasped Ana's arm. "We will find him," she promised. "And we will bring him back."

"Nothing can keep him from you, Princess," Griff said. "I have witnessed that myself."

Ana escorted them to the palace entrance, and watched them as they headed toward the beach, a calm acceptance coming over her.

She knew what she had to do.

After changing into one of the dresses in her wardrobe, she called for Milly and her handmaids to do her hair, then asked the guards to meet her at the front entrance for her visit to the beach.

However, she slipped out of the side door and headed down the gardens toward the beach alone.

Unfortunately, she didn't know how to create the raft. That was pure magic and not something she understood. Maddoc hadn't used any spell or items unique to him. As she walked along the beach, wondering where to find the magic sand, she suddenly realized it was all around her. Picking up a handful, she held her fist over the water and spread it out into the water the way she'd seen Maddoc do, and to her utter surprise and delight, rippling gold waves began to form on the surface, turning into a raft.

She climbed on tentatively, unsure how to direct it where to go. "Please take me to Maddoc," she whispered.

The raft began moving, speeding away from the beach, smooth and calm, and Ana sat down in relief. She hoped she ended up in Allandis and not somewhere else. She turned to look at the palace she was leaving, the new home that Maddoc had tried to create for her. But it wasn't a home yet. Nothing was a home without the people she cared for; she needed to be comfortable in order to embrace it.

Maddoc was a much more complicated man than she'd initially thought. Stubborn and irrational, he insisted on having his way, on having her, but he'd held onto information just like everyone else. She couldn't allow Maddoc to suffer for trying to help the people she was supposed to protect, the people her father was supposed to protect, and some answers she needed, only he could give. There was so much Maddoc hadn't said and so much she still didn't know. What was he hiding and why?

There were also some hard questions for her father and mother, including why she was so sheltered from the truth about the royal assembly and why she was deeply attracted to a man who wasn't her fated mate.

She turned to stare at the direction that she was going, and a fierce determination gripped her. She wouldn't stop until she got the answers she needed. It was time for her to grow up.

Within half an hour, the raft slowed at a lake near the honey marshlands, close to the palace. She climbed off and watched it melt back into sand, floating on top of the waves. On instinct she crouched and dipped her hand in the water to see if she could preserve any. The sand converged to the center of her palm, and when she lifted her hand out of the water the sand was dry. She grinned. So that was how they did it. Pouring the sand into a small pouch attached to her dress, she hid it among her skirts, then marched to the nearest town.

A royal sentry on the outskirts of the town stared at her as she approached, his mouth dropped open. "Princess Ana?"

"Yes," she said firmly. "Take me to the palace."

TEN

MADDOC

Maddoc held still as he leaned against the wall in a tiny closed-off corridor between the kitchens and the storerooms in the palace.

The pain in his shoulder had been getting worse, aching so badly he couldn't sleep. The previous day the pain started thudding through his body, and that was a bad sign. He had no choice but to continue on; his healer wasn't available and he couldn't risk anyone reporting where he was to the royal assembly.

It had been much easier to navigate the kingdom when no one knew what he looked like. Since his appearance in court to claim the Royal Promise, and his subsequent public visits to the castle, he was too easily identifiable. He couldn't risk traveling for too long out in the open or going to any of the healers who might have helped him when his healer was unavailable—just in case they reported him. Luckily, all the secret passages and spaces of the palace were still available to him and that was what he needed right now, even at the expense of cutting all communication with his highcloaks.

He had spent the last few days locating all the remaining members of his guild who hid in plain sight and helped him around Allandis. Some of them had already suffered, and a few had died, but that just drove him to push harder to get them all out.

The days he spent showing Ana who the houses truly were, other members of his guild worked to protect the ones suspected of being sympathetic to him and his cause. That was where the real danger was, because the royal assembly were doing whatever they could to force people to talk.

And it wasn't people like his highcloaks, who had the training to withstand interrogation. The people who helped him were just normal commoners, trying to live their lives peacefully and avoid being targeted by the assembly. They were usually grateful for Maddoc's interference with the royal houses' actions, having seen or experienced their devastation firsthand. Some of them were people he'd helped get back into society, some felt compelled to to join after seeing him step in. Others just didn't like the power the houses had and how they used it.

Regardless of their reasons, all of them had been loyal to him over the years and now they were dying, or having to watch their families and friends die if they didn't give up their knowledge about Maddoc and his highcloaks. He couldn't blame them. Allandis had a delicate balance, and his attack on the king had upset it. Some of those targeted weren't even his supporters, but got punished anyway—applying intense pressure to everyone was how the assembly finally managed to find out where Moonvale was. They were closing in.

Since the families had moved home, it had been quiet at the base. Memories lingered of the people he'd met, the families who'd grown and expanded, and everything that growth signified. It was the end of a long period of time in his life, and now he could move on. With Analisa.

Footsteps clunked past, only pausing when two sharp raps sounded against the wall. That was his signal. The last family he'd been looking for were in the palace prison, like he suspected.

Maddoc shuffled along the corridor, trying to determine the best way to get to the prisons without alerting the king's guard. In his current condition, he could possibly handle two or three of them, but with his injury, any combat was a risk. It was a struggle to even use a bow and arrow.

When he reached the end of the corridor, he pulled himself up into the overhead panel in the ceiling and crawled along the space to get to the other end of the palace.

His size and weight slowed him down. He couldn't risk alerting anyone to his presence, realizing there was someone above who could see and hear what they said and did.

It was when he was crawling over the entrance hall that he heard a voice that made him go cold.

"I want to see Duke Ryden immediately."

Analisa. Maddoc froze. What the fuck was she doing in the palace? She shouldn't even be back on Allandis mainland! Shifting himself so he could look through the panel, Maddoc's annoyance spiraled. Maybe what he'd said to her hadn't sunk in. Maybe she thought it would be easier to challenge the crown from the inside? But either way it meant that she had left the protection of their home. Fury gripped him hard, but he couldn't do or say anything from where he was. If Ana was back in the clutches of the palace and the Royal Court, it would be hell trying to get her out again.

But he would do it. He didn't care how often he had to try or how long it took; Analisa would be with him. And this time, he would take the opportunity to kill that fucking Duke.

Overhead, he followed Ana as she went to the throne room where Ryden sat. Maddoc navigated to his normal space behind the lattice wall at the very top of the room, watching from his obscured view as Ana approached. As usual, she looked stunning. He grit his teeth hard, annoyed that she was wearing one of the dresses he had provided, and she'd styled her hair in the typical elaborate way of the court. The last few nights had been almost impossible without her, but he'd been looking forward to going home to her.

"Ana." Ryden had the decency to at least sound relieved. "We have been so worried about you, being captured by that savage, yet again. I'm so sorry I didn't take your warning seriously. But no one could have guessed what he was going to do at the wedding, nor what he did to your father."

"Where is he?"

"Who? Your father? He is in his chambers."

"I mean Maddoc."

"I don't know."

"Ryden," Ana snapped. "Where is Maddoc."

Ryden was silent for a moment. "We have spoken before about your tone with me, Ana."

Maddoc tensed. He couldn't wait to kill this bastard.

"Those rules are not for me," Ana said. "They are for your Omega."

Ryden shifted in his chair. "You are my Omega or have you forgotten that? Has he fucked you so hard that you've lost sight of who you are?"

"Actually, yes," Ana said, a smirk in her voice. "But that is not my point."

Maddoc's brow rose. Did Ana just admit enjoying fucking him to the duke?

"We have been lied to, Ryden. We are not fated mates."

Maddoc gripped the wall, his muscle tensing as pleasure, satisfaction, and relief bounded through him. She knew. She finally knew.

"What do you mean?" Ryden asked evenly. "We have been betrothed for years."

"But we do not have the attraction that fated mates should have."

Ryden was still in his chair for a moment and then leaned forward. "You are not exactly the most experienced woman, Ana. How do you know?"

"Because nothing and no one else should feel more powerful or as intense," Ana said. "I may not be very experienced, but you are. When you were with me, when you kissed me, did it feel that way to you?"

"I'm not sure how I see that that matters at this current time," Ryden said curtly.

Ana peered at him. "What?"

"What difference does it make?" Ryden stressed. "I enjoy sex, you clearly enjoy sex, it makes no difference if we are fated or not. That's just an added bonus to help couples rule equally."

"So you don't care about it?" she asked, puzzled amazement in her voice.

Ryden leaned forward. "I don't care about ruling equally, Ana. I never have. Your parents did a good job. They raised you to be gullible and ignorant and reliant on myths and legends about Alphas and Omegas so you would be bendable to my will—they made it easy for me."

"Easy for you to do what?" The edge of Ana's hardness returned.

"To rule alongside an Omega who won't want to assert her will, or interfere with things she knows nothing about."

Ana's shocked silence lasted only a moment. "So you know what's been going on out in the kingdom." Her eyes flashed. "You knew what was going on, yet you did nothing to stop it! Don't you care about the people? What is the point in being king if you're not going to do something about the people's suffering, Ryden?"

"I had an idea what was going on, but not everything," Ryden said. "I avoided looking too deeply into it until I could actually do something about it."

"So becoming king… that was your goal? So you could stop the atrocities?"

"Partly," Ryden said. "I cannot deny that I relish the idea of setting laws and ruling the kingdom. But yes, I do want to stop what is happening with the houses. But it cannot be done the way the outlaw is doing it. Violence against violence is not the answer."

"Then what is your plan?" Ana said sharply. "To sit here and make policy and law without ensuring it is used correctly?"

"I told you that your father was unfit," Ryden said sharply, pointing at her. "You refused to see it."

"You didn't tell me exactly why he was unfit. You gave Maddoc as the reason."

Ryden inclined his head. "Yes, because once you knew, it would be a never-ending series of questions and nagging about doing something about it. I will do things in my own way. You do not understand the powers the houses have. They will only put someone on the throne who will agree with them. Changes have to be small and made bit by bit."

Ana shook her head. "And in the meantime many suffer."

Ryden exhaled and leaned back in his chair. "Listen, Ana. Your idyllic view of life is not reality. I'm sorry that it's turned out that way for you, but it is the reality for everyone else. You have to take your place in it and deal with your new responsibilities and what is to come."

"My responsibilities?"

"Yes. You are still betrothed to me. You are still my fated mate in the eyes of Allandis, and we are still to be married."

Maddoc almost growled out loud. Why couldn't this Alpha get it through his fucking head?

"You can either choose to do so willingly, or you can be forced."

Ana frowned, taking a step back, and at that Maddoc did growl.

"What do you mean?" she said.

Ryden rose from his chair. "You are the rightful heir to the throne, Ana. Whoever marries you is king. It is not so much a choice as it is your duty to choose someone who will stop what the houses are doing the *right* way. And if you don't, then you will be forced to by law."

"So, you'll create some random law that says that I have to marry you?" Ana snapped.

"You have already been betrothed to me for five years. Redcrest is owed something for that commitment and devotion, and they know it. So it's better that you are willing."

Ana was silent for a long moment as she stared at him in horror. "You just care about the crown and the throne."

Ryden didn't bother to respond to confirm her words.

Ana shook her head, rubbing her fingertips against her forehead as she thought. "Why did you really go to Sterling?" she asked. "Why did you see Leoma."

Ryden grinned. "I see you are starting to think like a real human being," he remarked. "And not a doll."

"Fuck you," Ana shot at him.

"You will. You will many times, Ana."

Maddoc held in the roar that rumbled in his chest as he maneuvered himself across the space. He didn't need to hear any more. He needed to get down there and take his Omega.

"You went to House Sterling to see if you could marry Leoma, didn't you?" Ana asked, evenly. "If you don't believe in fated mates, it doesn't matter which Omega you have—especially when I was potentially going to be sullied by the outlaw and you were thinking about your options."

"Correct. But that doesn't have any bearing on my preference for you, Ana," he said, smiling. "You are prettier, and your training makes you much more suitable for royal events. But, if your reputation was going to be ruined by the outlaw, I was considering other options. Unfortunately, Sterling wanted too much control of the crown in return for her."

Maddoc slid out of earshot as he entered the corridor. Peeking through another panel, he waited for the approaching footsteps to pass, but they stopped outside the door. Then he noticed their black cloaks.

He jumped down from the panel.

Raine's sword snapped up, and Griff was already lunging with his dagger. Maddoc dodged them both, grabbing Griff's wrist just before he was stabbed. The other three highcloaks already had their arrows notched.

"Maddoc!" Raine's face lit up.

"What the fuck is Ana doing here?" he said, trying to keep his voice low.

Griff frowned. "Ana is at home, Maddoc."

"She's in that fucking room, Griff," Maddoc said, jabbing a finger at the door. "Didn't you keep someone on her? Just because the kingdom is safe doesn't mean she wouldn't leave."

Raina groaned. "I should have known she would," she murmured, shaking her head. "She was worried about you. She wanted to come and we said no."

Maddoc ignored the satisfaction and pride that bloomed at his Omega's independence. So she came for *him.* But it didn't help that she was now in immediate danger. "They going to arrest her so they can force her to marry," he growled. "We need to go in and disable Ryden and collect Ana. We need to get Elizabeth and her family too. That's why I came here."

"Elizabeth?" Raine asked. "From the house on the duke's mansion grounds?"

"Yes. They are in the prison."

Raine's nostril's flared. "I'll help here and then I'll get them."

"We will too," Griff said.

"Elizabeth is the last of our people," Maddoc said. "So as soon as you have her, go straight home."

Everyone nodded, and they all faced the door.

Maddoc braced himself, ignoring the increasing ache in his shoulder. This was it. Everything that was worth fighting for was in that room, and he would either take her back home with him, or he would die.

Eleven

ANA

Ana glared at Ryden as though she was seeing him for the first time.

Every word that came out of his mouth infuriated her to such a degree, she wished she had learned some kind of combat training so she could show him just how docile she felt right now. Ryden wasn't bothered about correcting what was happening in the kingdom immediately; he only cared about power, and he wanted it by any means necessary, even if it meant deceiving her into marriage and trading their children.

She thought back to all the times they had spoken—it had been a minimal amount of times during their long engagement—and there had never been an urgency or thrill or desire between them. He was simply the man who she was to marry, and she'd been excited about the prospect of marrying, to have what her parents had, but she'd never been excited about him. How could the pairing process have failed?

Or maybe it didn't. He implied that her parents had purposely raised her to be this way, but he didn't make clear if they were complicit. She had to know. "Did my parents know about your plans?"

Ryden smiled. "Of course not. I'm sure they suspected something, but I doubt they were too concerned about it. They were too busy concealing their own deceptions."

Ana narrowed her eyes at him.

"So which is it?" Ryden asked. "You marry me willingly or we have a forced marriage?"

"I will never do anything with you willingly," Ana spat.

Ryden chuckled. "I'm sure if you ended up wet and willing for the outlaw, there is plenty you'd be willing to do for me. I guess we shall see." He turned to the king's guard at the door. "Arrest her."

Ana firmed her stance and prepared to fight. Ryden hadn't even confirmed whether or not he had Maddoc, but it was unlikely he did. He would have already boasted about it and probably announced it to Allandis. That meant Maddoc was still out there. And he would be coming for her.

Just as a guard reached her, the door banged open, and Maddoc strode in with Raine, Griff, and two other highcloaks. Ana's relief was so immense her knees weakened.

"You will never have her," Maddoc bellowed, his sword drawn.

"It is *you* who touched what is mine," Ryden shouted. "You are too late in your attempt to claim her."

Maddoc readied his stance, but Ana noticed his injured arm was limp. "You never even had a claim in the first place."

The guards, Ryden, and the highcloaks charged at each other, roaring, yelling above the clashing swords, whipping of arrows, and exchanging of blows. Since they were all experienced fighters, all of them moved quickly; jabbing, turning, thrusting, pivoting with precision and deliberation. The king's guard nearest Ana grabbed her and pulled her back to the wall, pinning her wrists together.

"Release me," Ana demanded. "I am the rightful heir to the throne. You work for the crown, not any one man."

"I'm sorry, Your Majesty," he said. "But the regent king has givin me an order, and I cannot disobey."

"Did you hear anything that we just discussed," Ana said, incredulously. "I know you all hear everything. You must know what is going on in the kingdom—what he is letting happen."

"Yes, we do hear everything," the knight said bitterly. "But we are sworn to the crown never to repeat a word of it."

Ana twisted her body to look at him. "You are loyal to the crown? To my father?"

The man nodded. "I have been in service to the crown for fifteen years, Your Majesty."

"Do you think the kingdom will improve with Ryden on the throne?"

The knight was silent for a long moment. "I do not have a choice in the proceedings regarding the throne," he said finally. "I only serve it. We are trained to accept this and not take action simply because of our personal wishes."

Ana eyed Maddoc. "That may be so, but Maddoc is my fated mate. And if you are still touching me when he comes over here, he will run you through with his sword. And you would have died for *this* king." She glanced at him. "For restraining the rightful king's daughter."

The guard thought for a moment and then released her, taking a few steps back.

Maddoc and Ryden parried, but it was clear that Ryden was more agile, given Maddoc's shoulder injury. Once she'd dispatched of a couple of guards, Raine joined Maddoc, both fighting Ryden, and the speed they moved at was unbelievable. At some point, Ryden realized that Maddoc was injured, and he landed a blow on his shoulder joint.

Maddoc bellowed, drawing back at the same time Ana yelled out for him. Maddoc saw her and started to inch around the room to get to her.

But Raine did not stop. Ryden narrowed all his attention on her and as they fought, both of them intensified the battle. The size difference between them was almost comical, but where Ryden relied on brute force, Raine used skill and agility. Each fighter was incredible to watch.

Maddoc dispatched of the rest of the knights as he made his way around the room, careful not to get in the crossfire. Ana kept her eye on Raine, marveling at how strong she was, how fierce she was… This was not what they taught Omegas at the palace. And suddenly her mind made the connection. Ana blinked. If Raine was an Omega, why wasn't she part of the royal assembly?

Suddenly, Raine's sword was knocked from her hand. She immediately grabbed Ryden's outstretched wrist and knocked his sword out with her knee. Ryden grabbed her and they grappled, falling to the floor and rolling before stopping with Ryden on top, pinning Raine down.

"No!" Ana cried.

But as she watched, Ryden lowered down, looking at Raine more closely. "You are a girl," he exclaimed as he panted, almost in disgust.

"I am a woman," Raine growled back.

Ryden grabbed the neck of her tunic, looking down her top. "A little woman." He stared at her. "Who are you?"

Raine did not answer, struggling underneath him to be freed. He grabbed her neck to keep her still, and then, much to Ana's shock, lowered and ran his nose up her neck, scenting her.

Maddoc reached Ana and grabbed her, lifting her into his arms. She hugged him fiercely, relief flooding her body, and she pressed kisses all over his mouth. He pushed her against the wall and kissed her properly, dominating her mouth like he always did. Ana moaned as she savored his taste, every hair on her body standing up as she inhaled his familiar scent. Damn, she had missed him.

"I thought you'd been captured," she said breathlessly, when he released her.

"That is not an excuse to leave home and put yourself in danger," Maddoc growled, his hands roaming her body. "Did any one touch you?"

"No." She twisted to look back at Ryden and Raine on the ground, still watching each other, tense with animosity and curiosity. "Ryden," she called out. "Let her go."

Ryden straightened, dragging his head away from Raine's, even as he kept her pinned down. "Who is she?"

"None of your fucking business," Maddoc bellowed. "How many women do you need?"

"How many do *you* need," Ryden thundered. "I assume you're claiming that one," he pointed at Ana. "Why do you have this one? Who is this? She is clearly an Omega. Is it herbs that have interfered with her scent or is she damaged?"

Ana's breath left her. How could he tell Raine was an Omega?

Maddoc groaned under his breath and Raine suddenly spurred into action, kicking and punching as hard as she could to get him off her.

"Just let us leave, Ryden," Ana said. "Let us all leave."

Ryan looked back down at Raine and then slowly got up, dragging her with him.

Griff and the other men had left the room, so it was just the four of them and the knight remaining.

Ana turned to the king's guard, who'd released her. "In times when a regent king is disputed, a separate guard can be formed to protect the needs of the crown. I need fifteen king's guard who will listen to me and take orders from me as priority over the regent king, in the name of the integrity of the crown. Would you be one, and can you find fourteen more?"

The knight glanced at Ryden and nodded.

"Good, please bring them here," she said.

"Clever," Ryden said. "But they need to pledge to a representative of the crown."

"Let Raine go," Maddoc warned.

Ryden made a face. "Raine?" He glanced at Raine. "What kind of name is that?"

Raine scowled at him and tried to pull away again from his grip.

"Are you planning to declare yourself queen and marry him," Ryden asked Ana, pointing at Maddoc. "Because that would be a mistake."

"The king lives," Ana said. "I don't need to declare myself anything. You will not marry me and that means you will not really be king unless he dies. And even then, there are many Alphas who will want the throne and they are more experienced than you. What makes you special?"

Ryden scowled. "We have already been betrothed for years," he said. "If you default by not marrying me, then Redcrest is owed a debt by the crown, and all I would need to do is collect on it is to use your own crown's guard."

That was true.

At that exact moment, guards entered the room.

"Your job is to protect the crown at all costs. King Orick is the rightful king. He must be guarded constantly and is never to be left without a member of this guard by his side. Anyone who tries to harm him dies immediately. I order this as heir to the throne, Ana of Allandis; however, you are required to pledge an oath to be a representative of the crown." She glanced at Ryden, who looked upon her smugly. "The king did not rule alone. He was part of an Alpha and Omega couple, one of the most powerful ruling couples that are recognized by this kingdom. So you will pledge your oath to the only remaining official representative of the crown, Queen Atara."

The guards nodded. "We will pledge immediately."

"That will not last," Ryden snarled as they left the room. "I am the regent king. They have to listen to me!"

"You can be acting king, Ryden," Ana said, realizing she had no interest in the throne. Once the new guard was in place, she didn't have to worry about the crown. The weight of years of training and protocol and expectations was suddenly lifted, and she felt weary. "I don't care anymore. I don't want to rule this corrupt kingdom. If you want it, you can have it. But you will not take it illegally or unjustly. Father is still king, and when he fully recovers he will decide how things will move forward."

For the first time, Ryden was quiet.

"If you do well between now and then, you will have the ruling experience no other person has had," Ana added. "It is your best chance at gaining and keeping the throne honestly."

"I will agree to this if you let me have her," Ryden said, gesturing to Raine.

"I am not for sale," Raine shot at him.

"What house are you from?" he said. "Where have you been all this time? You are too pretty to be living rough like an outlaw."

She glared at him, not saying a word, while Maddoc growled. "She will not be your whore, Ryden."

"I don't need whores," he shot back. "We need another Omega in the royal assembly."

"What for?" Ana said.

"Leverage."

When Ana shook her head, he scowled. "Then I will do everything I can to kill you, your father, your mother, and eliminate anyone else who gets in my way. Do you think I won't succeed with at least one of them? I haven't been making efforts for years, taking painstaking steps to reach this stage, only for you to get in the way. So make your decision."

Ana opened her mouth, but Raine held up a hand. "It's all right, Ana." She turned to Ryden. "I will join the new guard. I will be here every single day protecting the king. I will answer any questions I choose to answer, I will not join the royal assembly. But as soon as the king recovers, my duty is over."

"No, Raine," Maddoc said.

Raine gave him a look. "We are almost there, Maddoc. Our home exists, your mate is with us, and we got everyone out. But it will never end if we don't make a compromise. You and Ana will never be safe at home if he is here plotting and scheming against you both."

Maddoc was silent for a long moment. "You know what is coming."

Raine nodded. "And if I am here, the king has a better chance of surviving."

Ana glanced between them, unsure what they were talking about. "Raine, I appreciate you making this offer, but you don't have to do this. You deserve to be home, too, like the rest of us."

Raine smiled at her. "I can't sit and twiddle my thumbs, remember?" she said, grinning. "This is just temporary and then I will come home."

Ryden turned her to face him, and she yanked herself away hissing. "You will not manhandle me!"

Ryden's thunderous face held as he glared at her, and he dragged her toward him. Ana was about to push out of Maddoc's arms to go to them, but Ryden suddenly chuckled and let her go.

"It will certainly not be boring having you here," he muttered. He picked up his sword, looked at Ana and Maddoc. "What do you mean something is coming?"

Maddoc and Raine exchanged a look.

"At least two other kingdoms will join forces and invade Allandis within the season," Maddoc said.

Ana snapped her head to him, her face going cold. "What?"

Ryden stared at him. "Two other kingdoms? *Two*?"

"Why would they do that?" Ana asked.

Ryden expression darkened. He raised his sword and pointed at Maddoc. "You did this," he thundered. "You organized it!"

"I cannot control two different kingdoms; tell them to combine resources, leadership, and then conduct an invasion," Maddoc said firmly. "They are doing it because the houses have strayed into their lands with their abuses."

Ryden did not respond—he seemed speechless.

"How do you know this?" Ana asked.

"I told you. I monitor anyone and anything that does not belong here," Maddoc said. "The other kingdoms have been watching us for a long time."

Ana nodded, recalling the men who had ambushed her father. "The men with the different insignia."

Ryden found his tongue. "When?" His voice was hoarse. "When is this happening?"

Maddoc shrugged.

"What are the kingdoms called?" A growly edge entered his tone.

Maddoc shrugged again.

Ryden gripped his sword, his mouth tightening. "Fuck!" Shooting Maddoc a look of murderous fury, he left the room.

Ana finally relaxed in Maddoc's arms, her body trembling with the sudden release of tension.

"I'm going to introduce myself to the new guard," Raine said. "One of them will have to pull back." She smiled at them both. "I'll see you before you leave."

Ana nodded at her, as did Maddoc. "Thank you, Raine."

As Raine exited, Maddoc pushed Ana up against the wall, reaching under her skirt.

"Maddoc!"

"I wanted to be inside you from the moment I came in this room," he growled, ripping off her panties.

Ana already knew that. She'd been able to smell it in his scent. She hummed with delight as he widened her legs, batting away her skirt so he could claw her ass as he pressed into her. There was a desperation for both of them to connect in the purest way they knew how. "Someone might come in," she whispered.

"Good," he murmured. "Then they will see you are mine."

As he filled her up, stretching her wide, she tucked her head into his neck, breathing in his scent. "I missed you so much. You said you were coming to the kingdom."

"I was," Maddoc groaned. "I just needed to get everyone out. I promised them they would have a new home. They helped me and suffered for me."

His cock sunk into her so deep and stretched her so brutally wide, Ana could barely breath. "I understand," she whispered.

Maddoc pulled her head from his neck to look at her. "Do you?"

Ana searched his eyes. "You are not the man they say you are. I understand that. You care very much about the commoners, and that is something we share. But there is much you still haven't told me. I don't understand why."

Maddoc held her eyes. "Because it has no bearing on who we are together. This feeling between us, Ana. It should be what leads us."

"But it is the lies and the secrets that made me ignore it for so long," Ana whispered. "I couldn't understand it, and I rejected it. I don't want anything else withheld between us. If I had known the pairing process doesn't work—"

"It does work."

"It cannot," Ana insisted. "It paired me with Ryden."

Maddoc growled, flicking his hips, and Ana's body jerked, the strange pain of being filled so deep shooting to a peak. "Do not talk about him when I'm inside you."

Ana leaned forward, eager to comfort him, her nose nestled in his neck, and he rumbled in satisfaction.

He pushed in even deeper and slowly withdrew to the tip only to slam in again. Ana's toes curled as he fucked her slow, steady, and hard as if savoring every inch of her. She licked his neck, sucking on it as he grunted, loving the sweaty taste of him.

Maddoc sped up slowly, each thrust sweeter, and wetter, and sharper than the last, until Ana was humping her hips for more, tortured by his rhythm. Her orgasm built in crashing waves, layer upon layer of feral, sinful, and violent devastation, assembling perfectly only to break and shatter her while she screamed and convulsed. He was still fucking her when she went limp, all muscles exhausted except the ones clinging to him between her legs, unrelenting in their greedy need for more.

His tongue was in her mouth when she came, making her swallow his gruff barks and growls, connecting another opening that he dominated completely. He slammed his knot in hard, and Ana yelped, but the primal contentment of his knot in her while his cock jerked inside filling her, spread quickly.

Maddoc carried her over to the throne, and sat on it, wrapping his thick arms around her as she lay on his chest, sleepy and exhausted.

"I was born into House Sterling," Maddoc said.

Ana jerked awake. She didn't move, just opened her eyes and listened.

"I was a promising member of the royal assembly and always took my duties at court seriously. I wanted to be a knight but my father was a scholar. He thought I could be much more—a man who used brain and brawn to reach heights others struggle to get to. So while I started my combat training, he pushed me to study and examine and research everything. I read a lot. I wrote reports and investigative research, and aimed to learn as much as I could.

When I was thirteen, my father told me he had uncovered a series of bribes and exchanges that unfairly advantaged Redcrest to keep hold of the throne."

Ana lifted her head. "What do you mean?"

"There are five houses. Those five and the crown make up the royal assembly. But the crown is a separate entity—it has no specific association with any house."

"Yes," Ana agreed.

"The king and queen can come from any of the royal houses, and when they take the position, they lose their family name, and become wards of 'The Crown.' So, if someone from Thorneshaw becomes king, he can no longer have allegiance to the Thorneshaw families and he can no longer use the name."

Ana nodded, resting her head back down.

"The problem is, one cannot just turn off the feelings for their family members or family friends. It is always the case that whoever rules will slightly favor whichever house they came from. There were measures in place to stop this from becoming a serious hindrance to the system, but ultimately there's always a slight favoritism. One way the favoritism issue is dealt with is nominating Alpha and Omega couples to rule the kingdom. By doing so, a house is more likely to have a ruling couple on the throne if an Omega was born into one of the families."

Ana nodded. That was how she understood how things worked.

"For the longest time, Sterling and Redcrest both had a lot of ruling couples on the throne, which is why they are the wealthiest houses. But at some point, Redcrest began to cheat. My father found evidence that they went to great lengths to acquire Omegas—to guarantee the couple on the throne would continue to favor them. The longer this went on, the more biased the favoring became.

"When I was thirteen, my father found evidence. It included , including the recent story about your great-grandmother and he was preparing to inform the other houses so it could be corrected. Before he could share what he had learned, he was killed by Redcrest knights. I saw them with my own eyes.

"I tried to save Father's research, so I could expose them and have them pay for what they did, but they took it a step further. They killed my mother, my aunts and uncles, my cousins, everyone. They eliminated the entire family so Sterling lost a complete family. And then they blamed me for it."

Ana's breathing slowed to a standstill, her heart beating in her chest. That was horrific. "And the other Sterling families believed them?"

Maddoc nodded. "I had none of the evidence. My father was the one who put everything together. So I became their monster from that day. But it was on that day, I was matched with you."

"Me?" Ana said lifting her head.

Maddoc nodded, his eyes holding hers. "I hadn't met you yet, but earlier that day the scholars told me that we were fated. I hadn't even seen you yet, you were really young, but they matched us very early, which means that we are incredibly compatible."

"But why didn't I know about it?"

"When my family was killed, I was painted as a villain, and all documents and reports, anything with my name was erased, including our matching. I was already a criminal avoiding the law and couldn't earn a living doing something useful and simple, but I quickly discovered how cruel the houses were being to commoners. They formally enslave commoners through taxes, Allandis Law, and duties while they enjoy the fine life and conceal what goes on. They make the rules so that they can break them but nobody else can. I soon found that I was the only one who could retaliate. I no longer had anyone they could harm and I had no livelihood.

"I will admit, I was as brutal as I could be in my retaliation, and the more I tried to help people, the more brutal I became. It was necessary to try to find a permanent safe place.

"When I heard about your wedding announcement, I remembered that we were matched, and I couldn't understand how you could be matched again. I'd left you alone because I told myself I didn't need you. It wasn't worth bringing somebody else into my world, and especially not someone aligned so deeply with Redcrest. But I thought I would at least see what you were like."

Maddoc paused, and when Ana glanced up, he was looking down at her, his beard twitching. "I fell in love with you the day I saw you. I knew I had to have you. So I started to look into you, and research who you were, and I was disappointed to find that you didn't have a voice. You were a mild-mannered ornament for the crown, but didn't seem to have your own opinions, even in court. I began to wonder if we'd really been matched correctly. But I knew by then I was going to take you anyway, because I couldn't let anyone else have you. You weren't ready for me, so I planned and waited for five years. By the time I got into the room with you, I had convinced myself that there was nothing behind the vacant shell that they had made you into—that they had ruined my gorgeous mate. But then, you insulted me, you slapped me, you refused me. And I saw *you.* It was the moment I knew everything had been worth it and anything coming would be worth it."

He lowered and kissed her, and Ana blinked away tears from her eyes. "I know I wouldn't have believed you if you told me," she mumbled. "But I wish I'd known."

"If we had had our three nights, you would have."

Ana squinted her eyes at him. "How? What was so important about the three nights?"

Maddoc gently lifted her off his lap, and she winced as his cock slipped from her sore folds. "You will find out."

TWELVE

ANA

"Mother."

The queen lifted her head from where it rested on the king's bed. Her face was haggard and exhausted, and for a moment Ana worried for her health. She sat in a chair next to Father's bed, holding his hand.

Ana." Her mother smiled when she saw her. She stood and reached for her, pulling her in for a hug. "I didn't think I'd see you again. How did you escape? Are you doing well?"

Ana hugged her back, looking her in the eye when she withdrew. "I am, despite the actions you and Father took against me."

The queen's face dropped. She lowered back down to her seat. "Nothing we did was to harm you, Ana. I hope you understand that."

"You were going to have me marry a man who I wasn't fated to. You forged the match so that I wouldn't question marrying him. How could you do that?"

"Would you have preferred to be an Omega that never had a fated mate?" Her mother said, her brows drawing together. "Do you know what kind of life that would be for an Omega?"

"But I did have one."

Confusion flickered in her mother's gaze and then died. "Who?"

Ana crossed her arms. "Don't pretend that you didn't know, Mother. You knew I had a fated mate."

Her mother swallowed. "I suspected that it could be someone…. The only person ejected from the assembly. But I had no way to contact him, and even if I did, I wouldn't want him for you."

"It wasn't your choice."

"It was," her mother said sharply. "We had a responsibility, Ana. We had to make sure you were matched so that you could take the throne. The scholars couldn't find any mate for you, and that was terrifying to us. We had to do something."

Ana shook her head. "I don't understand. Why was it terrifying? Why wouldn't I be able to continue if I wasn't matched with a fated mate?"

The queen inhaled, closing her eyes for a moment. When she opened them, tears glistened, but Ana ignored them. She wouldn't be manipulated any longer. "Your father wanted us to start explaining things to you much earlier, but I couldn't." She glanced at the king, lying still on the bed. "I just thought if we could get past your wedding to Ryden and then…." She gestured to the other chair next to her. "I will explain everything now."

Ana glanced at the door where she knew Maddoc was waiting. She'd had to be stern that he not enter while she spoke to her parents, so that she could find out the truth, but she knew he wasn't happy about it. He'd only reluctantly agreed because his healer, Agnes, wanted to look at his shoulder, but he said he would be coming back to get her immediately. She sat down, her eyes on her mother. "I don't have long."

"Our family have a long and distinguished history with the crown," her mother began. "But that is not an accident."

"I heard." Ana muttered.

Her mother ignored her. "We are Redcrests, and we have been on the throne for at least eight generations now. Our ancestors have done terrible things to the other houses so they could remain the dominant house that provided kings and queens to the throne. They abused the structure of the royal assembly; I don't know why. I assume it's because of greed. The crown aligns itself with Redcrest and sometimes Thorneshaw, but it eventually it became clear to the other houses that Redcrest had a stranglehold on the throne. But by then there wasn't much they could do."

"Why didn't you and Father do something?" Ana asked. "You could change things, turn everything back to how it was supposed to be."

"I would have loved to do that, Ana," the queen said, her smile wistful. "But too much animosity has built between the houses now. Serious life-changing incidents and events have affected the houses. It's not a matter of apologizing and moving past it. Once a Redcrest no longer holds the throne, the house and its families will be made to suffer. It doesn't matter that we are not the people who committed those crimes in the past, we will still be made to pay. Sterling, in particular, is waiting for their chance to eradicate us, and they have the power to do it once we no longer control the throne." Her mother gave her a knowing look. "I'm sure if you're aware of some of things we did to them, you can guess how they may choose to retaliate?"

Ana chewed the inside of her cheek. "So it's important to all the Redcrest families that a Redcrest remains on the throne."

"Yes, it is crucial. Unfortunately, I could only have one child."

Ana took a sharp breath in, her eyes snapping up to her mother's.

"And that child had to be our heir." The queen held her gaze, tears trickling down her cheeks. "Your father and I, and the entire house of Redcrest were so relieved you were an Omega. The only thing left to ensure was that you had a fated mate."

"Why? I could have ruled with a husband. I still would have been the heir."

The queen shook her head. "No. Because two of the houses also have Omegas. If they found their fated mates and you didn't, they would argue that their Omega has more right to the throne."

Ana exhaled.

"So I prayed the scholars would match you, and when your seventeenth birthday came and they hadn't I was worried. The earlier the match, the stronger the bond. So I asked the scholars, and they said they had nothing yet, but there was still time to match you—until you were twenty-one. But I didn't want to risk it. I did some research, followed up on some documents that I found, and I discovered that soon after the incident that happened that caused a man to be ejected from the assembly, the scholars of that year were all murdered."

Ana's jaw slackened. "Why?"

"I don't know," her mother said, shaking her head. "It was carried out quietly, and most of them were made to look like accidents. I didn't think it was strange when I was looking into it, until I noticed that a pairing had been completed when you were five; it was never announced." She lifted her shoulders. "There was no documentation, so I didn't know whose names were there, but the only reason to destroy it and anyone who knows about it, is if it would affect the crown."

"But why wouldn't they just let it be announced? I wouldn't have had a mate, and they would have gotten what they wanted."

"No, it would've been an invitation to your mate to come and claim the throne. In the time it took you to grow up, your mate could rehabilitate himself, make arrangements with another house... anything could have happened. And no one would have wanted that. It was better for it to be announced that you had no mate, and then another Omega could be selected from a different house."

Ana scratched the bridge of her nose as her frustration spiked. If the houses spent half the amount of time caring about the commoners as they did the throne, the kingdom would be in a better state. "So you did decide to forge my pairing with Ryden?"

"Yes, I realized that it was unlikely you would ever be with your fated mate, and it gave us the opportunity to choose. And we chose to the best of our ability."

"You chose someone who only cares about the crown," Ana said sharply. "He didn't care about me at all. To him, Omegas can be exchanged and bargained for, as long as they are quiet and obedient. He wants an Omega who has no opinion and who will let him do whatever he wants. He doesn't care about the Alpha and Omega relationship—he doesn't want it or believe in it. That is what you would have subjected me and the crown to."

Mother's gaze dropped. "Yes, that was one of the reasons your father and I chose him."

"What?" Ana's breath became shaky.

"How could we choose someone who would desire something they'd never get, Ana? We couldn't. And we couldn't let you discover what the real connection was like."

"That's why you hid the books," Ana whispered.

Her mother nodded. "We didn't let anyone use the library when you were in it so you didn't accidentally come across it. Milly was told that I would be in charge of that area of your growth, and since I am an Omega, she never questioned it. We thought we had it under control."

"But you were the biggest example of it, Mother," Ana said, unable to stop the tears filling her own eyes. "You and father showed it to me every day. I loved the way you were with each other, and I watched you all the time. I would have eventually known that what I had wasn't the same."

"Eventually," her mother agreed, with a sad smile. "When it was too late to do anything about it." She wiped her tears. "The fake pairing, the lack of books, limited contact with others, especially Omegas, encouraging you to feel duty-bound to the crown... all of these things would have ensured success, Ana."

Ana exhaled heavily, unable to believe the lengths her parents went to deceive everyone and maintain power for at least another generation. "I cannot believe you would do all this! And to your own child!"

"I would rather do this than have you and your father dead," her mother said, sharply. "Or savagely tortured for years on end, paying for others' crimes. We had to do what we needed to so we didn't suffer at the hands of others, Ana. But I admit, it all came from my failing. Omegas are supposed to be the most fertile of dynamics, and I couldn't give your father more children. The weight of that failure presses heavier each day."

Ana glanced at her father. "He knew about it all, and agreed to it?"

Her mother nodded. "Recently, he wanted to tell you."

"Why?"

"He... had doubts about you spending your life with Ryden. He wanted you to have what we have, if it was a possibility."

Ana swallowed. "So he knew what Maddoc was to me?"

"Not as first. We just thought your mate was somewhere out in the kingdom. Neither of us had any idea that *he* was the man who'd been ejected. We only realized it after you left, and Maddoc wanted to chase after you and keep you. He didn't behave like the sordid opportunist he did in court."

“Did Father really make a deal with him?”

The queen nodded.

Ana leaned back in her chair thinking over what her mother had said, hardly able to believe that almost all of her life had been constructed to protect a lie. Lies upon lies. She felt hallowed out, empty from all the shameful and vile actions taken by the people who were in control of the kingdom. “When will it end?” she murmured.

Her mother's gaze returned her father, lying on the bed with sallow, sweaty skin. Her voice almost a whisper. "The houses have ruined this kingdom. They used to stand for so much, they used to mean something, and now they have ruined it."

"Do not blame the houses," Ana snapped. "You are the queen, you are the crown, you had control over what they do. You could have taken steps to stop them."

"The houses are supposed to work with the crown," the queen said, a bitterness in her tone. "The crown cannot function if every single house is corrupt and working against it. That is not its purpose. It is supposed to be the conduit for the work of the houses, otherwise you will have one couple who controls everybody instead of channeling the needs of the many into one focused aim to help everyone. It is the houses who are out there among the people. We rely on them for guidance about what the people need. We cannot be everywhere to know what is happening all over the kingdom," she exclaimed. "It’s enormous." She shook her head. "There is only so much anyone can do."

Ana nodded, tears coming to her eyes at the realization that she had been lied to about everything her whole life, more deeply then she even thought. The crown was not powerful; it was weak to the houses, and as long as the houses were corrupt, there was nothing the crown could do. She realized why Maddoc didn't have a problem with an invasion. It was the only thing that might interrupt the abuse of the houses. And that was the only thing that would give her hope.

Ana rose from her seat. "Mother, I am going away. I've left someone in the new guard who can communicate with me, but I'm leaving Allandis to be with Maddoc."

The queen smiled up at her. "I know, Ana. And I'm happy for you. Your father will be ecstatic. When he recovers, he will want to see you."

Ana stepped closer to the bed and leaned down to kiss her father's cheek. "I'm sure he would," she said, as she rose. "But I'm not sure if I will have anything to say."

The queen grabbed her arm. "Everything we did was for our preservation, Ana. I'm sorry that you had to go through all those falsehoods, but it was necessary."

"No, Mother, it wasn't." Ana patted her arm, and turned to the door. "Maybe if you had put more value and faith in me, I could have helped. After all the studying I did, I probably know more about Allandis law and history than most."

Her mother squinted at her. "What do you mean?"

Ana turned back to her. "All you had to do was disown the crown and the Redcrest name, and no danger would have followed us. But you didn't think about that, did you? Nothing was more important to you than the crown. Even me."

❖

The sight of Maddoc waiting for her in the corridor saved Ana from descending into the heavy depressive mood that infected her from the conversation with her mother.

He immediately pulled her into his arms, as if he could feel her distress, and she couldn't help the sobs that overcame her. He pulled her close, comforting her from the disheartening, brutal, and bloody truth behind the royal assembly. Her life had never been her own—it had never been real, not until Maddoc entered it. He'd been a destructive force that she'd hated at the time, but he was the only honest and authentic element.

She cried for the life she had and for the loss of who she thought her parents were. She cried for the omegas who would be manipulated in the same way, and for the children who would take on the burden of their parents' actions. But most of all, she cried out of relief that she was free of it. She had Maddoc, and she finally understood that he was her Alpha. He had already shown her the life he was prepared to provide for her, the life he had planned for them, and nothing could be more comforting than that.

"I do not like to see you cry," Maddoc rumbled, dissatisfaction in his gritty tone.

Ana wiped her tears. "I'll be all right. I just can't believe how terrible people can be; the people I love, the people who are supposed to stand for something."

"I learned that early," Maddoc remarked. "But we don't have to be concerned with them anymore, Ana. We are starting something new. That is not our reality anymore."

Ana nodded, smiling. "I know. And I'm glad for that."

Raine approached them in the corridor. "I arranged for a carriage to take you to the nearest body of water," she said. "I suggest you leave soon. I don't want anyone causing trouble for you." She shot Maddoc a disapproving look. "Do not do anything but rest when you get home."

Maddoc glared back at her, as though affronted she would tell him what to do.

Ana looked between them and laughed.

"Don't give me that look," Raine said warningly to Maddoc. She turned to Ana. "Agnes said the poison in his shoulder could have been fatal if she hadn't treated him today. He needs to look after himself."

Ana sobered, looking at Maddoc. "Why didn't you see her to heal you?"

"I didn't want to take her from your father. I know he is important to you." He held her gaze. "And I was not lying in court when I said I don't want him dead, Analisa. I want him alive for what is to come. He shouldn't escape it."

Ana lifted her head in understanding. He wanted Father on the throne for the invasion. "But why didn't you tell me that he was alive and being treated?"

Maddoc held her gaze, holding her tight as if afraid she might escape. "I never intended for you to see your father again after our three nights. I thought it would be easier if you grieved for him."

Ana breathed shallowly. “Why not?”

“They tainted my claim on you, Analisa,” he said, his voice harsh. “They worked for decades to achieve a goal that involved twisting your mind against your own nature. So much so, you didn’t recognize what I was to you. I cannot allow their rot to infect everything good we have, and hope to have.”

Ana lowered her eyes and nodded. She couldn’t argue with his point. She didn’t know if she would ever trust them again. Never seeing them again would be hard—they’d been all she’d known—but she would rather not see them at all than risk them destroying anything else in her life.

Raine placed a hand on her arm. “I’ll keep you updated with their progress while I’m here.”

Ana smiled at her. “Thank you.”

"There are some healing lakes at home that Agnes said he should use every day for a week,” Raine said. “Please make sure he goes.”

"I will." Ana said, grinning at Maddoc.

"Thank you, Ana," Raine said pointedly.

Maddoc scowled at them both.

Ana leaned over to hug Raine. “Thank you so much for joining this guard to look after my father,” she said. “I know it’s a burden and you don't know how much I appreciate it, especially with the invasion coming."

"You are very welcome," Raine said as she squeezed her back. "I was worried about being bored at home, but now, at least, I get to spend some more time honing my skills here. There isn’t much better training than the royal guard."

Ana pulled back to arm's length to look at her. "Be careful of Ryden."

"I can handle him," Raine said, a snarl almost forming on her face. "I'm not going to let him control me just because I'm an Omega."

"That's not what I mean," Ana said. "It takes a lot to surprise him, and I think he was surprised by you today, a great deal. In fact, he seemed speechless. I don't know how he knew you were an Omega, but he's pretty smart. He will try to figure you out."

"That's the only thing that worried me," Raine said, biting her lip. "He seemed to guess I was an Omega just because of my size and looks... I don't know how."

"Sometimes Alpha's can tell," Maddoc said. "It doesn't happen often, but you were in a high stress, pressured combat situation. He may have sensed something on an instinctual level. Ana did too, so it's worth being careful. Maybe you need a new bracelet."

Raine nodded. "All right, I'll be careful."

After saying their good-bye, Maddoc and Ana made their way out of the castle and straight into the carriage. They traveled to the honey marshlands, where Ana trickled the sand into the water to create the raft.

"How are you feeling about magic now?" Maddoc asked, as they climbed on.

"I believe!" Ana laughed. "I'll have to do some more investigations about it." She cuddled into Maddoc's chest as he tucked her into his lap, then reached up to kiss his cheek. "Thank you for Milly. And for the library, I love it."

He chuckled. "I knew you would."

"I love all the Alpha and Omega stories. I'm going to read them first." She looked up at him. "How did you get everything over to… What do you call that place?"

"It's called the Buried Kingdom."

Ana made a face, and he chuckled.

"That's the name it was given when it was first found," Maddoc said. "But we can name it."

"Who found it?"

"Many people have discovered it over the centuries," Maddoc said. "It is extremely difficult to detect and shrouded by powerful magic that cannot be controlled by any individual. It is well hidden."

"It is," Ana agreed. "But where exactly is it? Are we in Allandis still?"

"Yes, it can only be accessed by Allandis, and no other kingdom. But no one stays there because it is too separate and cut off from any of the other kingdoms."

"Is that a bad thing?"

"In general, yes," Maddoc said. "For trading and entertainment and the intermingling of people and produce, it is too closed-off for it to be sustainable in the long-term."

"But it is suitable for us?"

"Yes. since we have people from all over the kingdom—all different districts and different backgrounds—we can thrive in a place like that. We've already done it with Moonvale," he said. "I know it will be successful. I just didn't want to move everyone over until we were all ready. Now I have you, we are ready."

Ana flushed, and Maddoc pressed a long kiss on her lips. "So, with the invasion coming, no one will try to take the kingdom from us?"

"No," Maddoc said. "All records of how to get there have been destroyed. Plus if anybody did find out, or accidentally traveled there, there is only one way in and out, and they will face numerous highcloaks if they arrive."

"So we are really going home?" she asked, leaning back and closing her eyes.

Maddoc's purr began deep in his chest, the vibration rumbling through her body, and a pure, potent serenity glided over her, coaxing her own purr into existence.

"If you are with me," Maddoc murmured, "you already are."

THIRTEEN

ANA

Arriving back at Buried Kingdom with Maddoc was a completely different experience than when she had first arrived. When the raft threw them against the shore, dissolving around them, Maddoc pinned her down on the sand, kissing and nibbling on her lips as he told her that it was customary for the king and queen of the kingdom to fuck on the entry beach when they first arrive together.

Ana raised a brow and laughed. "You made that up!"

Maddoc pulled away with a stern expression, even though his beard twitched. "Every declaration I make here is law."

"How can I be queen?" Ana asked, still giggling. "I am not married to the king."

"We are fated mates, Ana," he rumbled, this time completely serious. "It doesn't matter if we are married or not. All my people know that you are the queen of this kingdom, and that you will lead them."

“Is that what you told Trea?" she said giving him a look. "You seem to have been talking about me to her quite often."

"She is very forceful," Maddoc said, irritably. "But also very cute."

Ana burst out laughing, rolling away from him on the sand. "You cannot say no to her, can you?" she teased. "She has you soft for her."

"No," Maddoc scowled as he pulled her back to him. "That is reserved for one woman only."

Ana's laughter faded and she lifted her hand to brush her fingers over his beard. "I don't think I could ever control you," she murmured.

"You already have for five years," Maddoc said, lowering to press his lips against hers and he pulled off her panties.

When they finally made their way to the palace, Maddoc explained that he had known about the palace from a mention in his father’s research. After discovering Allandis was unbearable for so many people, he started looking to it as a possibility.

Surprisingly, almost everything was brand new. Maddoc had taken builders, inventors, and engineers to the kingdom to start creating the palace five years ago, and although the city was already in existence, it was severely rundown, many of the houses crumbling or in ruins. The work began slowly because he could only depend on the people who joined the guild, but the more commoners who joined, the quicker the work was completed. They were very enthusiastic about the work, because they knew they were creating and building their home.

"So not everyone from Moonvale came here before?" Ana asked, as they entered the palace.

"No," Maddoc said. "Most people supported us by staying where they were in Allandis and putting up with the assembly so they could keep us abreast of developments and provide support. The ones at Moonvale couldn't stay in the mainland of Allandis for various reasons—mostly because their lives were threatened. They usually had a skill or trade they could contribute, and even if they didn't, they were willing to work or learn. It was only the people who had the skills to build this who came here originally."

"It's a very impressive palace," Ana said.

"The whole kingdom is impressive," Maddoc said, a tinge of pride in his voice. "I have to show you something." He grabbed her hand and led her through the palace to the library. "Wait," he muttered. "Here first." He navigated her to a room at the back that he hadn't yet explored. Inside portraits hung on the wall. Ana stepped closer examining them. They looked familiar but she couldn't recall where she'd seen them. It was only when she saw her mother that she realized they were portraits of royals. Similar to the ones in the library in the other palace, but these were so lifelike. It was almost as though they were looking directly, the artwork composed to show the subject's character.

She stared at all of the different ruling couples in the royal family and farther along the wall were portraits from the five houses. Ana was surprised that Maddoc would have them up here.

She stopped in front of a portrait and gasped as she leaned forward. That was Maddoc!

She looked up at him grinning, but tears stung her eyes. He was just a grinning boy in the portrait. No darkness in his eyes, no beard, just floppy hair and a great, intense smile.

"I was thirteen then," Maddoc said from next to her.

Ana ran her finger over his cheek. "Before everything happened."

He made a noise in the back of his throat.

Next to him was his father, who Maddoc as an adult resembled greatly, and all the members of Sterling who had been murdered.

"Are you sure you want to keep a record of this?" she asked him, as she walked along. "I am upset about all that has happened. Knowing what my life was about to become because of many of the people on this wall."

Maddoc encircled his arm around her. "It is still fresh for you, Analisa. One day soon, it won't feel this way. But we cannot allow ourselves to forget any of this—any of them. It is part of our history. It may be uncomfortable, but it is what made our life together possible now."

Ana pursed her lips, glancing up at him with doubt. "I can't see a day when it won't be sensitive to me. So much of it is horrific."

"I know," Maddoc said. "But our children will also need to be aware of what happened. If they decide to leave this kingdom and travel to Allandis one day, they must know what they are dealing with."

Ana nodded in agreement, trying to hide the flush up her neck. He'd never said anything about children before, but something within her was delighted.

“Over here.” Maddoc led her back to the library, leading her over to the back.

Next to one of the shelves was a square platform with rigid sides that looked like a large basket or carrier attached to cords of rope hanging from the ceiling.

Ana examined it and looked up. "What’s up there?"

Maddoc stepped on top of the platform and pulled her with him. He touched the rope, and the whole thing lifted up into the air.

Ana squealed, grabbing onto Maddoc to secure her. Watching as the floor drifted farther away. She looked up and saw that they were heading into an opening in the ceiling that she hadn’t noticed before. She glanced at Maddoc, but he leaned against the edge of the basket watching her, his beard twitching.

As they ascended through a narrow column, Ana realized that they were traveling up into one of the spheres of the building she had seen from outside. The round circular teardrop structures at the top of the towers of the palace building was what made the palace so unique.

When they reached inside it, Maddoc stepped off, pulling Ana with him as he took her along the sphere, and opened a doorway to a flat roof. Ana stepped out and gasped at the sight before her.

They were high above the palace and were able to see in every direction; the kingdom spread out far and wide, beautiful in the afternoon sun. Maddoc pointed out the city where the Moonvale families lived. He pointed to a sea where he wanted to teach her to fish and a forest where he wanted to go hunting, as well as more spaces to expand on their city.

"We are small, but we will grow," Maddoc said, wrapping her in her arms.

"This is beautiful Maddoc," Ana said breathlessly. The rush of being so high up made goosebumps flare all over her. "I've never seen a view like this before."

"Yes, and you can read from here," Maddoc said, gesturing to where seats and a low table had been placed for her.

Ana smiled at him, her tears almost blinding her. "I love it."

❖

Ana wasn't the only one thrilled that Maddoc was in the kingdom. It seemed that the entire palace was in a state of excitement that both of them had arrived, and therefore their life in their new home could truly begin.

Milly was clearly nervous about meeting Maddoc, but remained composed as he greeted her and asked her how she was settling. Afterward, she admitted she would need to get used to pushing aside the prior memories and knowledge of him, especially from the court hearing that started everything, but she was glad she was here.

"Do you know," she added, "when you're together, the two of you are just like your parents."

Ana smiled but a melancholy mood gripped her. "I know."

The next few days, Ana got to know the palace and its staff. She discovered that many of the handmaids and household staff were women from Moonvale or Allandis, who had traveled here with their families. They didn't have any training to work in a palace, which meant they didn't follow what would normally be expected of palace staff. Ana found it refreshing and finally made some friends, of all ages, who she could laugh with and learn so much from. Of course, Milly didn't allow too much tomfoolery and scolded Ana along with the staff. As head of staff, she was constantly whipping them into shape.

The first night Ana and Maddoc spent in the palace, they were able to indulge in each other for the first time without any restrictions. For Ana, it was the first time she submitted fully to being with her Alpha, without any thought of consequence or shame or regret. It was incredible. Maddoc dominated her so thoroughly, taking her in every way possible, twisting her body into a variety of positions so he could sample her pussy in different ways, she became a mindless bundle of instincts. She didn't let herself think—there was no need to—this was her Alpha. She licked and sucked every part of him, whined when he teased her or didn't give her what she needed and fed his cock into her pussy at every opportunity.

It was almost as though they were back in the room at the palace, except there was no limit to how far they could go. Maddoc fucked her all over the room just like he had then, but he really loved when she rode him on her toes, like she did in the healing tent. He lowered her onto his cock, sinking her down so far until she was completely filled with that amazing brutal burn. Ana moaned; her eyes rolled as her head dipped back. Maddoc kept his arms around her waist and worked her on his length, grabbing her ass to tilt her the way he knew she liked, the way *he* liked. His eyes were trained for when her hips took over, grinding and wriggling of their own accord, seeking that pleasure she needed. It didn't take long. Soon she was riding him so hard he growled and gripped her hair, leaning her back on him to watch her breasts jolt and sway with each movement. She loved when he watched her, and they fed off each other, both their climaxes savage and consuming.

The next night was the same; they had sex throughout the night, barely stopping to sleep or rest. The bedroom was saturated with their scents and the more time they spent together, the more they relied on their instincts. Ana woke the next morning in a nest she had build for them in the height of her need for him with blankets Maddoc had pulled from the cupboard.

On the third night, Ana finally discovered why Maddoc had always wanted his three nights with her. After an entire night being wrapped around each other, smeared in their fluids, buried in their nest, Ana woke exhausted and worn out; she snuggled up close to him only to find he smelled different. Her nostrils flared as his new scent worked through her body, sparking something deep and volatile within her, a primal force pushing her forward and stripping all thought from her mind except for her Alpha. As she climbed on top of him, he woke, his eyes carefully tracing her every movement. Without saying a word, he sat up and lifted her body, positioning her over his cock.

He held her there, his eyes so fierce, watching her as she wriggled her hips, seeking a fulfillment she didn't understand.

"What is happening," Ana panted, whimpering at her restriction.

"Just follow your instincts," Maddoc growled in that gritty low voice that made her gush. "Do whatever feels natural."

Ana moaned, spreading her legs wider needing more. "Do something," she pleaded.

"I think we have to wait." He glanced down at her pussy, licking his lips.

Ana pressed her thighs together, realizing he was right. She wasn't ready yet, but she didn't know what for.

It was another few agonizing moments before a pounding ache in her pussy made her gasp, but before she could say anything, Maddoc slammed her down on his thick, blunt length.

Ana screeched as multiple violent climaxes hit her at once, and at the same time Maddoc bit into her neck. She soared. Propelling through chaotic waves of euphoria and flames of merciless ecstasy, Ana could no longer feel her own body. When she finally came down, Maddoc was on top of her, pounding her into the bed, frantic and frenzied, still latched onto his claiming mark on her neck.

Ana squealed with delight at the feel of his teeth digging into her skin and clawed his buttocks as they clenched, needing more brutality, more pain, more domination. And he gave it all to her.

Hours later, they lay languid deep in their nest, hardly able to move.

"Can you feel it?" Maddoc asked.

Ana couldn't even turn her head to look at him, but she could feel the change deep in her chest. "What is it?"

Maddoc chuckled. "What does it feel like?"

Examining the feeling closer, it was strong, heated, sensual, and trapped in her ribs. It was powerful, intense, primal, and most definitely Maddoc. "You," she said in surprise.

"Good. I feel you too."

With great effort, Ana propped herself up on her elbows. "Is this what you wanted to happen on our third night? For us to bond?"

"Yes."

Ana wrinkled her nose. "But I hated you back then."

Maddoc drew her to him. "But you wouldn't have been able to stop it. We both would have had no choice. And you would have known immediately how I feel about you."

Ana looked up at him. "I thought bonding could only happen during an Omega's heat or marriage."

"That is true for most people," Maddoc said, brushing her shoulder with his lips. "But our match was recognized very early. We have a stronger connection than most. If you continue to read the Alpha and Omega books, you'll see that before the scholar method, this was the method to determine a lot of fated mates. Going by how attracted they are to each other over three days. But it only really works for the ones with strong connections like us, so they refined the method."

Ana played with his hair, sinking into deep thought. "So if we had our third night, we would have been bonded? And then you would have convinced me to leave the palace with you?"

Maddoc lifted up onto his elbow to look at her. "No. Once we bonded, you would've been able to feel how much I already loved you. And why I needed to take you. And whatever happened after that, would have started from there."

❖

The bond took some getting used to.

Maddoc's feelings were so dominant that sometimes Ana mistook them for her own, but she loved that he was so closely connected to her. He could be at the beach while she was in the city and they would know each other's moods and feelings, sometimes even thoughts. She didn't have to tell him if she was tired or irritable or content, he just knew. She felt how much he wanted to kiss and touch her, making her blush. Her friends in the palace teased her constantly about it; they could always tell when Maddoc was about to come around the corner in an aggressively aroused state and carry her off to their bedroom.

Ana found herself happy beyond anything she could imagine. She suspected even her parents never had such a connection, and she wished they had given up the throne so they could truly experience each other the way she and Maddoc did. The kingdom was flourishing each day, and her heat was imminent, which meant Maddoc was making all efforts to get her pregnant. She was looking forward to it.

Sometimes she found Maddoc on the library roof, looking out over the kingdom quiet and solemn, and she knew he was still processing that dark side of himself he had reveled in for so long. He had spent years killing people, just as brutally as the houses, and Ana knew it wasn't something he was comfortable with, even if it had been a worthwhile cause. So she sat with him, comforted him with her presence, touch, and sent support and encouragement through their bond.

"I love that you understand, Analisa," he said one evening on the roof, as she climbed into his lap.

Ana snuggled into him. "I spent so long not understanding, Maddoc. It is time for me to do that now."

Maddoc rumbled, pulling her closer. "That doesn't matter. All that matters is that you are with me now. In our kingdom, with our people, in our home. Soon you will be with child. It's what I always wanted."

Ana thought about her parents' love, how she aspired to have that for so long, and yet she never could have imagined that she would have so much more. She smiled as she looked over the kingdom. "I couldn't have even dreamed of this, Maddoc," she whispered. "My eyes were closed to the possibility of having this."

Maddoc kissed her, squeezing her tighter to him. "That's why I dreamed it for you, until you could see."

Epilogue

Ana

Ana pulled back the string of the bow, feeling it grow tight and dig into her fingertips as she adjusted her aim at the thick oak tree. Holding her breath, she released the arrow and watched it soar. It veered so far to the right it shot past the tree with over a foot of distance between them.

She dropped her arms and cursed. After finally getting the arrow to actually shoot, instead of limp off the bow, now she couldn't get it go where she wanted it to. She reached for another arrow, determined to hit something, but stopped when anger and relief flared in her chest quickly followed by heavy footsteps approaching from behind.

"Analisa!"

Ana turned to see Maddoc storming towards her, tense and agitated. She smiled. "Morning."

Maddoc swept her up, her pulling her into him as if desperate to get his hands on her. "You will not leave our bed while I am sleeping," he thundered, tilting her back to glare at her.

Ana blinked at him. "I didn't want to disturb you."

His arms tightened around her. "I intend to waken every morning looking at your face. I do not permit you to leave my side at night."

Ana reached up and stroked his cheek, twisting her fingers into the thick hair of his beard, and rubbed her thumb along his chin. He calmed, but his baleful glare remained. "I didn't mean to worry you," she murmured, leaning forward to nuzzle him. "I just love it here in the mornings. It's so quiet."

Although they'd explored as much as they could of the new kingdom, Ana found herself returning to the forest more and more. It felt alive with excitement and mystery, and in the mornings, the pink-tinged sunlight beaming through the trees calmed and settled her mind.

Maddoc breathed heavily, his gaze on her smile as his body finally relaxed. He looked down at where she'd sat and peered at the bow. "Why are you using this? Isn't this one of Raine's?"

Ana nodded. "I want to learn."

Maddoc growled, picking up the bow and quiver, and started walking back to their palace. "You will not be learning archery, Ana."

"Why not?"

"Because you're not," Maddoc said firmly. "You will not be learning how to use weapons. That is not your role here. I will not have you getting hurt."

Ana glared at him. "I won't get hurt! It's not like using a blade. Bow and arrows are simpler." Her frown dropped as she remembered her failures all morning. "At least… I thought they were," she sighed.

"I can assure you archery is not simple," Maddoc said. "It requires specific technique and cannot be learned successfully without good tuition."

"Then maybe someone can teach me?" Ana suggested.

"No."

"Maddoc!" Ana twisted in his arms. "Why not?"

"I told you already," Maddoc said. "It's dangerous, and you don't need to. That was never something we agreed on."

"I didn't realize I had to make an agreement with you about how I live in this place," Ana snapped. "I thought we could both do whatever we choose and discover new things."

"There are some things that are obvious," Maddoc growled. "Discovering you with a weapon in the forest on your own is not something I ever planned to happen."

Ana's mouth tightened, but she said nothing more, growing stiff in Maddoc's arms as he exited the forest.

"You can be as annoyed as much as you like," Maddoc snapped. "You're not doing it. The baby needs you."

Ana narrowed her eyes at him. "So I can only do one or the other? Be a mother or learn to shoot an arrow?"

Maddoc glanced at her. "No. You need not choose. I just told you you're not doing one of them. Ever."

Ana huffed, an annoyance smoldering in her chest she knew he could feel.

By the time they reached the Palace both of them were in a state of heightened agitation. Ana wriggled out of his arms and marched away down the corridor, but Maddoc followed her, grabbed her arm and forcing her to a halt.

"Where did you get that?" he asked incredulously, staring at her clothing.

Ana glanced down. She forgot that she was wearing the layered clothing typical of Maddoc's guild—tunics and pants with boots. "It was a gift from one of the families."

Maddoc's jaw clenched. "You may return it."

"I will not!"

Maddoc's eyes darkened, and he lifted Ana back into his arms and started walking in the opposite direction. Ana fought against him, but he held her too securely.

"What's wrong with me wearing this?" she cried as he entered their bedroom and began undressing her. "You and your guild wear it all the time."

"You are not a member of the guild, Ana!"

He put her down, twisting and turning her until he had peeled every piece of clothing off. A beam of arousal shot through their bond.

"So I can't be part of your precious guild?" Ana shot at him. "Is that what you're saying?"

Maddoc grabbed her head and forced her to walk backward to their nest, his eyes dropping to her heavy breasts as his arousal climbed steadily in the bond. "That's exactly what I'm saying."

"Maddoc!" Ana growled. Before she could say any more, she backed into the bed and Maddoc forced her down onto it and climbed over her, his scent so powerful, she couldn't ignore it any longer.

"You are a mother and my queen," Maddoc said, parting her legs with his knee. "You are not a warrior or an archer or anything else that requires you to wear those clothes, Ana."

Ana struggled against the tide of desire and arousal that swamped her, both her own and his. Usually, she submitted to it, riding the wave of carnal pleasure and satisfaction it caused but she couldn't let it distract her this time. "I can be all of them," she said, through gritted teeth. "There were queens in the past who had combat skills and they—"

Maddoc's growl cut her off. He lowered to lick up her neck, circling his tongue over his claiming bite, and a violent shudder embraced her. Before she even knew what she was doing, her hands were on his pants, freeing his length and caressing along its shaft.

"Maddoc," she moaned, squeezing and rubbing as his fluid moistened her palms. "It's not…"

He kissed up to her chin and delved his tongue into her mouth. And all thought was lost.

By the time Maddoc and finished kissing her in his beautifully brutal way, she was guiding him between her open legs and pull him down on her. She gasped when he entered, filling her up as she twitched and writhed. It was always so unbelievably intense, so raw, so magnificent. Ana whimpered as he pounded her into the bed, reveling in his scent, the rhythmic sound of their wet joining, and his tongue on her neck. Nothing was ever this good.

❖

When Ana woke, she was disoriented. It took a long moment for her thoughts to straighten, but once they did, determination gripped her again. She would not be a slave to the bond.

Untangled herself from Maddoc, she pulled back on the clothes Maddoc had taken off her. Picking back up the bow, she slipped out of the room and headed to the nursery.

When she peeked in, she saw Milly rocking the baby in a chair by the window. "How is she?" she whispered as she approached.

Milly grinned. "Sleeping. She is a good one. She's been no problem since you left."

"Let's hope she stays that way." Ana propped the bow up against the wall and slumped down in the chair next to Milly. "I didn't get to do much this morning."

"I'm guessing Maddoc was not that enthusiastic about it?" Milly said, giving her a wry smile.

"No," Ana scowled. "He told me he 'forbids it.'"

"You're not surprised, are you?" Milly shot her a knowing look.

"He's being unreasonable."

Milly raised a brow. "And you're not surprised, are you?"

Ana sighed. "No. Raine said he didn't want her to train either. But she's amazing now. You should see her fight, Milly. I've seen nothing like it. She's as good as Maddoc."

"How did she convince him to let her?"

"She said she wouldn't let him tell her what to do," Ana said.

Milly laughed quietly. "Well, I don't think you're going to have much success arguing that point, Ana." She rose and placed the baby in Ana's arms.

The baby stirred, but eventually settled in Ana's arms.

"I know," she grumbled, tracing her finger along her sleeping daughter's cheek. "But I don't understand why he's so against it. It would be better if I learned."

Milly tilted her head. "I thought you didn't like bow and arrows? You said they reminded you of your wedding, and your father."

"They do." Ana said, nodding. "But if I have to learn something, I'd rather learn that. And I realized I don't want to forget what happened."

Milly nodded.

"And besides, it's different when I'm in control of it…" Ana grimaced. "I'm not saying I'm in control of it yet."

"Why doesn't he want you to learn it?" Milly asked.

"He doesn't want me to learn to fight.".

"He probably won't ever let you enter battle anyway," Milly admitted. "So it's probably pointless."

"I don't care," Ana muttered. "It's not pointless to me."

Milly laughed. "You two are just as stubborn as each other. Don't tear the kingdom down while disagreeing about this. Or your bed," she chuckled, winking.

Ana couldn't help but smile. It was true. She and Maddoc couldn't argue without ending up in their bed. A strange compulsion happened when their scent changed that they both couldn't resist. The bond made every emotion more powerful, and she was still trying to make sure it didn't overwhelm her like it had earlier. She wouldn't let the bond give Maddoc an advantage over her when she wanted to do something.

"I'm going to go back out."

Milly raised her brows. "If you think it's wise…"

As she got up to hand the baby back to Milly, she woke, and Ana leaned in to kiss her. "Good afternoon, Lu. Mama's going back out to train."

Luella blinked up at her, a toothless grin lighting up her face. "You're the only one enthusiastic about this," Ana said softly, grinning at her back. Ana glanced up at Milly. "Wish me luck."

❖

She only made it as far as the edge of forest before she felt Maddoc's anger spike again. She ignored him, setting up her bow and arrow, and practicing until he arrived. She was sure she could stand her ground if they were outside of the palace.

But she didn't even hear him approach.

Huge hands swept her up, and before she could even scream, a tree bark pressed into her back.

"Explain to me why you are out here again, Analisa!" Maddoc demanded.

"I already told you," she said as soon as she could catch her breath.

Maddoc exhaled in frustration. "Why are you putting yourself at risk like this? Don't you realize you don't need to?"

"Then what am I good for?" she snapped.

Maddoc frowned. "What do you mean? You are queen. You lead and guide the guild alongside me and we make sure everyone is happy here."

"But I don't know about to be that," Ana shot back. "I've never known. I wasn't really taught how to be a queen, not really. If I don't learn to fight, I cannot defend our people; I cannot fight to help defend our child."

"You don't need to," Maddoc insisted. "Others will do that—it is not your job."

"What is my job?" she said, tears threatening. "Everyone has a role here, everyone knows their responsibilities and duties. They all have skills they use to make valued contributions to our community, and what do I do, Maddoc? I cannot do anything!"

"You are the most valued person we have, Ana," he said fiercely. "You may not have been prepared to rule in Allandis, but you are prepared for ruling *our* kingdom. We are starting anew, and your view of the world is what we needed to make sure that we can succeed." He exhaled a heavy breath as he looked down at her. "Do you think I don't know that we will eventually have crimes here? Or disputes and problems with some of our people as we grow and expand? It's impossible for us to remain without all the things a normal society would experience. And you have all the knowledge, Ana. You studied Allandis, you know its history, you know its failings and its weaknesses, but you also know it strengths. And you are the one that needs to guide and lead and protect us. But you can't do it with a bow and arrow!"

Ana clung onto him, tears streaming from her face, unable to come to terms with her fear. "Why can't I just try? What harm will it do?"

He paused for a moment, as if trying to find the right words. "Preparing yourself to fight isn't just about learning a weapon," he said finally. "Being skilled is just the start of it. It is also about how you use the weapon, how you expect other person going to use their instrument, and then you have to consider your surroundings, and ways you can attack and defend yourself. Sometimes you cannot prepare for what your opponent may do."

He lowered his gaze to her, his eyes soft as he took in her tearful expression. "And above all, you have to be prepared to kill them if they will not stop attacking you," he said. "I have seen many times—someone thinking their training truly prepares them for battle, but they are not really ready to take that last strike. And they ended up wounded or worse because of it. And that is why I am not allowing it, Ana. You will need to prepare your mind to kill and you don't realize the consequences of it. You are not like the highcloaks. You did not grow up witnessing what was happening in the kingdom, you did not have years of seeing or being a part of that kind of violence. I don't think you realize how much it will affect you. I don't want that for you."

A sob escaped Ana's throat as she realized his intention. He wasn't trying to restrict her—he was trying to look after her, to make sure she didn't have to experience what he had.

Maddoc gazed at her, the frustration in the bond draining away. Pulling her off the tree, he gathered her into his arms and cuddled her close. "Where is this coming from, Ana?" he rumbled. "I've felt your strange mood in the bond since you had Luella, but I thought it was because you were tired or getting used to motherhood."

Ana shook her head, scratching away tears that trickled from the corner of her eyes. "I just..." She swallowed. "What if I get it wrong?" she murmured. "When Luella was born, I held her, and I looked down at my beautiful tiny baby, and for the first time I could understand my mother's fear for her family, And I was scared too, Maddoc." Her voice lowered to a whisper. "I don't know what I'm doing, and I don't have my mother to help. I don't know how to raise our daughter to be strong and smart and capable—especially when I am not those things."

"You are," Maddoc said sharply. Turning, he headed out of the forest. "Those feelings are normal," he said. "Everyone fears for their children. It doesn't mean that you are incapable of raising them properly, Ana. We all have to do our best, and you are not alone. You don't have your mother, but you don't need her. You have me, you have Milly, you have all the families to help you. But most of all, you are an Omega. Of all of us, you have the best instincts to raise our child."

Ana took a deep breath, wiping her tears away. "I couldn't tell you were my mate, Maddoc," she pointed. "And I love her too much—I love you both too much—to harm you the way my parents harmed me. Well-intentioned, but harmful nonetheless."

As the last of the sun's rays streamed through the trees, Maddoc carried Analisa to a small area where the sun's golden light pooled on the ground, and sat, crossed legged in the direct heat. Fixing her in his lap, he tilted her face up to his, the warmth of the sun and the feel of his body calming her.

"Ana," Maddoc murmured, kissing her lips. "Your instincts told you I was your mate. They told you loud and clear. You just didn't believe them."

Ana bit her lip. That was true.

"You are not that sheltered Ana from Allandis you once were, not anymore," Maddoc continued. "You are not part of any Royal Assembly or a Redcrest. You are my mate, and my wife, and the mother of my children. You are loved and respected and your opinion matters to everyone here." He stroked her cheek, and the tension deep within her that had build in the months since Luella was born unraveled. "You need to trust that we will make the right decisions together, Ana."

Ana exhaled slowly, her fear and worry draining out of her. He was right. She couldn't let her old fears dictate the new opportunity they had. This was the chance for her to be the Ana she wanted to be, and she could choose what that was.

Lifting her arms and wrapping them around Maddoc's neck, she kissed him slow and long, breathing in his scent and moaning at the way he squeezed her ass. The simmering arousal that had sparked when he first lifted her up exploded between them, and Ana knew they would not make it back to their bed. As he yanked her tunic down, growling in search of her nipple, Ana made her choice. She wouldn't be a warrior. She would be a loving mother, a devoted mate, and the kind of queen Allandis had always needed but didn't get.

Ana smiled against Maddoc's neck as he lay her on her back, pushed up her tunic, and sunk into her, that delicious burn taking her breath away. She would be the woman she was always meant to be, with the man she was always meant to be with.

And she would enjoy every moment.

The End

Thanks so much for reading the Beholden Duet. The next couple in this world will be Raine and Ryden!

Author Note

Weeelllll. I have to admit that this story was extremely difficult to focus on during the last few months. I'm still not sure if I did the story justice to what I had in my head—I hope so! I really loved writing this couple. Thankfully, the world had already built organically from when I was writing the first book, and I am so pleased with how much it developed. This story started as a simple concept and then grew and expanded at a rate I wasn't expecting. I loved Ana and Maddoc's development and growth, and I would love to be able to revisit them. I already have ideas for two more couples in this world, but I'm not going to get ahead of myself!

Back in April (2020), I wrote an origin story for this world with King Allandis (mentioned in this book) to apply to an anthology, and it was a great exercise that had me thinking about the history of this world. That was probably the spark that made this world so potent in my mind that I was able to continue it. If that story is unsuccessful for the anthology, I'll be expanding it a little and making available to my Halos, so make sure you're on my reader's list to find out more.

The next obvious couple is Raine and Ryden, and when they finally met on page I was already laughing about how annoyed Ryden is going to be that he can't control fiery Raine. It will be SO much fun to write their story!

If you liked this duet, try my slighter darker Omegaverse series MYTH OF OMEGA series or my angel PNR series EMPIRE OF ANGELS. Thanks so much for checking this one out!

My reader's list Dark Halos is the best way to get news, bonuses, so sign up to hear about what's coming next!

Acknowledgments

Randie: What can I say? You are the most patient, kind, and generous person I've worked with. Amazingly talented and just so supportive. I'm so sorry this was all over the place, that's all on me. Thank you so so much.

Margarita: Raine, Raine, Raine… changed your mind, yet? Haha! Thank you for all the incredible support helping me through this one. It really made a big difference. Your enthusiasm and positivity and all-round general awesomeness is what helps when I'm flagging. And it makes all the difference to me. Thank you. We got this one done!

To my friends and family, I have never appreciated you guys more than in the last few months. I am so thankful for you all.

~ Zoey Ellis ~

About Zoey Ellis

Zoey Ellis writes dark, magical, fantasy romances about tortured, possessive, alpha anti-heroes and the sassy heroines who belong to them (even if they don't want to!). Filled with passionate, carnal steam, Zoey's stories feature couples that go through tough journeys and make mistakes but ultimately have to grow for each other to survive the dark worlds they inhabit.

Described as 'deliciously dark' and 'unputdownable', Zoey's thrilling, fantastical romances come complete with roller-coaster twists and turns, unique worlds, and happy endings.

Zoey is a Londoner, cat mama, and proud romance and epic fantasy addict. She loves jealous/possessive heroes, sexual tension that jumps off the page, and memorable, magical worlds. She reads most genres of romance and has a special love for the 'true mates' trope and dark angst.

Snoop around Zoey's online home for her favorite reads, release news, and bonus media about her fantasy worlds: www.zoeyellis.com

Printed in Great Britain
by Amazon

64619897R00158